Best

# THE
# PAPOOSE

## Alan Dunlop

*"When the white men came we gave them lands, and did not wish to hurt them… the white man… made us many promises, more than I can remember, but they never kept but one. They promised to take our land, and they took it."*

Chief Red Cloud
Oglala Sioux

# Dedication

In sincere and loving recognition of 56 years of generous, constant and sacrificial duty as my wife, and mother to our six children. Now Grandmother to 31 Grandchildren, and Great grandmother to Eloise, Texas USA.

A little encouragement may therefore be both timely and richly deserved.

*So if, my dear, there sometimes seem to be*
*Old bridges breaking between you and me*
*Never fear: We may let the scaffolds fall*
*Confident that we have built our wall*

From "scaffolding" by Seamus Heaney 1939--2013

The main character's association with Fetterman[1] at Fort Phil Kearny is fiction, as is the scene where he found the infant. However, the carnage described was an all-too-common occurrence in the measures taken to rid the land of the 'Indian Problem'.

Punitive measures exacted upon the indigenous population included the slaughter of women, children and the aged. Destroying their foodstuffs was an added evil, designed to bring about the most extreme hardship to any that escaped the massacres.

Fetterman's arrogance was legendary, as was his disrespect for the fighting abilities of the native population. That he did not survive more than six weeks in his new posting is hardly surprising. Custer's character also leaves a lot to be desired, as he too shared Fetterman's taste for slaughter. His disdain for the Indian, coupled with his own exaggerated opinion of himself, eventually brought about the deaths of his total fighting force at the Bighorn. The dead including two of his brothers, a nephew and a brother-in-law!

Spanning sixty years on the frontier, this book is merely an adventure story, yet one with a shocking insight into the daily realities of those momentous times. It is also a tender love story with a happy ending.

Language of the era is used throughout, without any disrespect to the memory of those who suffered such a colossal, cruel and catastrophic loss of centuries-old tradition and freedom.

The Indian Removal Act, May 28, 1830, signed into law by President Andrew Jackson, and pursued by subsequent presidents, marked the beginning of the permanent colonisation of America. This Act 'normalised', or 'legalised' as it were, the total subjugation of Native American people, and the subsequent brutalisation of the entire race.

History has not looked favourably on the measures taken, and the actions of those army 'heroes' who were applauded at that time for their exterminating zeal are now seen in a different light. Scholars and historians, now that the fog of war has cleared, are presenting facts long left hidden. Facts that are plain and clear, untainted now by gold fever, land-grabbing greed, racial prejudice or the need of geographical expansion.

Viewed through the eyes of historical research and discovery, it is clear that the development of America as we know it today was not achieved alone by social progress, pioneering sacrifice, or industrial and agricultural means, but all else was underpinned by brutality and bloodshed of heinous proportions, financed and orchestrated by a federal government intent on domination and expansion at all costs. The sad thing is that they found so many so willing to help them achieve that goal.

# CHAPTER 1

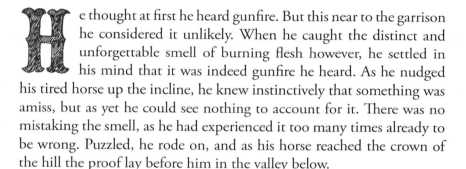e thought at first he heard gunfire. But this near to the garrison he considered it unlikely. When he caught the distinct and unforgettable smell of burning flesh however, he settled in his mind that it was indeed gunfire he heard. As he nudged his tired horse up the incline, he knew instinctively that something was amiss, but as yet he could see nothing to account for it. There was no mistaking the smell, as he had experienced it too many times already to be wrong. Puzzled, he rode on, and as his horse reached the crown of the hill the proof lay before him in the valley below.

As he drew closer, he counted around a dozen Indian tepees in scattered disarray, and the fires had already reached some of the bodies that lay within the tangled heaps. Ponies, two dogs, old men and women, children too, including infants. Whoever had done this did not want survivors. This was no Indian feud, no native dispute or tribal vendetta.

It was not difficult however to identify the marauders. A short distance away, on the fringe of the slaughter field, lay a cavalry mount. It had been stripped of its saddle and bridle, and a lance had brought it down. The haft was still protruding on either side of its once proud and well-groomed neck. Beside the horse an old man lay, sabre slashed beyond recognition. He had brought down the horse before he had been brutally killed.

Carson sat silently, allowing the scene to be etched on his mind. He counted the twisted and mutilated forms before him. From where he sat, he tallied 14 women and eight old men. The children, both male and female, numbered 16. It had been an autumn camp, such as was common in the Great Plains at that time of year, when women, and the feeblest old men, were left to prepare the pemmican[2] in preparation for the coming winter.

The greater number of children here was thus explained. These camps were a traditional and safe refuge for the very young, while the young men were on the last buffalo hunts before the worst of the winter brought normal life to a standstill. It was then, when the winter snows drifted deeply against the tepee, that the pemmican supplied the daily nutrition for the family.

Carson slowly walked his mount through the debris of broken humanity and noted that all the pemmican baskets, parfleche[3] and gourds, were slashed and destroyed. The racks of drying buffalo meat had also been pulled down; the meat ruined. Scattered also and trampled were the berries and nuts that would have been added to the mix. There would be no salvage when the tribe eventually discovered this carnage. This was not retaliation against warrior opponents, this was annihilation. A root and branch destruction of the innocent, their offspring, and their means of life itself.

A sight such as this needed no comment, but Carson's lips whispered one word, "Fetterman"[1].

He was just about to ride on when he heard it. Soft, but clearly audible, like a kitten's feeble cry of blind helplessness. It was curiosity alone that caused him to enquire of its origin. A dismantled tepee lay before him, and within its wreckage lay a young Indian girl. She could not have been more than 20 years old. Her once dark and shining eyes, now dull and empty, stared blankly at the sky above.

It was strange how the eyes told of a life already gone, Carson thought, as his own eyes took in the dark stain in the centre of her chest where the bullet had entered. A single shot from a trooper's pistol, a soldier's boast of 'Indian fighting' when he wrote home, a validation of his duty in the US Cavalry. The fact that she was a defenceless girl going about her peaceful duties would not be allowed to diminish the narrative!

He did not dismount, but taking his rifle from its scabbard, he used its muzzle to draw aside an old blanket, and as it fell back it revealed a sight that shocked even the hardened senses of the frontiersman. Under the blanket was an infant girl, the still fresh cord not yet cut and bound. This mother had been in childbirth when she was shot at point-blank range!

Dismounting quickly Carson gently detached the tiny mite. She was cold and still, but against all the odds she was alive! There was no time to waste and no other option but to take her with him. The child may not live, but he had to do what he could to save her now that he had found her. To him, life was precious, all life, and that included the most helpless and vulnerable. Unlike Cain of old, Carson felt he was always his '*brother's keeper*,' if and when circumstances called for it.

Opening his shirt, he gently placed the infant against the warmth of his own skin and closed both shirt and coat tightly to make it secure. He had no food to give her, but he could give her warmth, and warmth might just keep death at bay till he could provide better.

# CHAPTER 2

Carson's father Jason was a quiet industrious person, and came originally from the highlands of Scotland.

Due to a family scandal when he was still a child, which he felt coloured the villager's attitude towards his family, he moved south to Plymouth England, where he would be assured of anonymity, and a decent practice in the very busy seafaring community there. Jason Carson had been the first fruits of the marriage between Robbie Carson and Eliza McGarry. As he grew older the young man did not enquire as to the family scandal, and it was never spoken of in his hearing, even the mention of it was forbidden. Finally, taking his medical calling as his life's work, he gave himself to it and it alone, and determined to leave the past in Scotland and seek his future elsewhere.

In Plymouth, living close to the docklands meant that he was often called to assist when a ship came in, by reason of violence, sickness or disease. These shipboard visits opened up a door to his energetic and restless spirit. Tales came in from all over the world, but it was the tales from the New World that enthralled him. He was already tired of Plymouth. He was wearied with the sameness of each day and longed for adventure. At least a more demanding practice in more amenable surroundings.

Many and long were the evenings he and his young wife sat and talked over these things. She was an educated girl, a mill owner's daughter, and she knew she could easily find work if they went abroad, for teaching settler's children was always an open opportunity for those who were able and willing to give themselves to it. The matter came to a sudden conclusion one evening after the Carsons had entertained the captain of the latest vessel to arrive from the Americas.

The captain told of his ship hold carrying thousands of running feet of timber for industrial use, and many thousands of pelts[4] for the fashion industry. He said the timber he carried was cut from trees that made one dizzy just looking up at them. What a picture he painted of a land "flowing with milk and honey".

There was talk of gold too on the Great Plains. It was said that in the Dakotas, the Black Hills had gold nuggets lying on top of the ground, just waiting to be lifted. The only hindrance to date was the Indians, it was their Sacred ground and could not be disturbed. The captain went on to enthuse that all that was needed to unlock the treasures of this great bonanza was manpower.

Miners, trappers, farmers, storekeepers, teachers, doctors, blacksmiths, carpenters, wheel rights. There was no end to the skills that could be used in the New World, and skills that would make those that had them rich. He said those who were *game enough* to be *in first* could name their price and have the pick of the crop!

It was altogether too much for the young man, and in a few short weeks, he sold his practice and booked passage to a new life and fortune.

He negotiated a deal with a ship's captain whereby his medical services on the voyage would be greatly considered when it came to payment for the passage, and with the sale of his practice he purchased the many useful and necessary instruments, medicines, and supplies such as he might need in a frontier situation. Thus it was that Dr Carson and his young wife Helen arrived safely and expectantly on the shores that would be their final home.

The Carsons arrived in their new venture at the very beginning of a controversial political decision regarding the Indians. President Andrew Jackson[5] had just signed into law the Indian Removal Act, on May 28, 1830. By this, within the next 20 years, 60,000 Indians would be forcibly relocated 5,000 miles westward, away from their ancestral homelands, and all that they had formerly known and loved. Tens of thousands would die before they arrived there.

All this of course was still to happen, and the young doctor only saw in the legislation another opportunity for his services. He was accepted as a civilian surgeon, working for the army, and would travel with the company as far as Wyoming, where he would branch off northwest for the Powder River Country.

It was a most fortuitous circumstance for the man and his young wife. His passage across a rugged and dangerous terrain would now have the protection of the US Army, and expenses would be forthcoming also. However, the young couple soon had cause to ponder their previous elation, for the scenes that confronted them daily were to become a source of great sorrow and inner grief.

The Indians were ill-prepared for the rigours of such travel, and many died on the way, buried where they had fallen if buried at all. Their daily government ration of food had much to do with the fatalities, as two cups of hot water, some cornbread and a turnip could hardly be said to be marching rations.

Although the doctor was employed by the army, to care for army personnel, he always did what he could for the weary marchers when the opportunity allowed, but it could only be fleeting and secretive, as the watching eyes of the soldiers were quick to spot any deviation from the rules of the Relocation March.

Some soldiers of course felt for the Indians, and very much shared the sentiments of the doctor, turning a blind eye now and again to his missions of mercy. But they, like him, had learned too late that once the public allows legislation to pass into law, it becomes a weapon in the hands of the government, an all-powerful weapon, and thereafter no one is safe from its application.

After many months, and hundreds of cruel, rugged miles, the couple at last reached their point of departure, glad indeed to be parting from the daily sorrow that had begun to wear them down. Heading northwest towards Wyoming and the territories of the Great Plains, it was with new anticipation that the doctor took up the reins and urged his mules forward.

It was in the Powder River Country they would make their home, and the following year their first and only child was born.

# CHAPTER 3

e had no other name but Carson. He himself did not remember having another name, and so he was just Carson. Like many other incidents that shape lives and fortunes, it was a tragedy that brought about this unusual circumstance.

The frontier life had agreed with the young couple, and with the greatly increased inflow of immigrants to the Californian opportunities, as well as miners, settlers, farmers and trappers, theirs became an ever-growing medical practice. Helen never got to teach, her own son being the exception, for the need for doctor's services far surpassed all they ever imagined, and she became a necessary extra pair of hands in the practice.

Thus, it was from his mother's endeavours that Carson became literate, and, having no other reading textbooks, he was left with the family Bible as his one and only recourse day after day. From this early introduction to Scripture, albeit by default, he became quite a scholar in Biblical matters, and a source of great amusement and pride to his parents as he often stood on a low bench and *'preached'* to an imaginary congregation.

From the very beginning, as word spread that there was a resident doctor in the Powder River Country, the door to the doctor's cabin had frequent callers at all hours of the day and night. Gunshot wounds, mauling's by bear and cougar were commonplace among the trappers, and buffalo hunters and skinners had their own peculiar wounds and lost fingers.

Everyday domestic incidents accounted for many more. Tooth extraction, broken bones, campfire scalds and burns, bee stings, dysentery and stomach ailments. The list was as endless as the population was diverse, and Dr Carson's reputation among his own people soon spread as far as the Indian Nation. It became something of a legend that the white men had a medicine man even greater than their own! He smiled with amusement when told of the reputation he apparently had, but as far as patients were concerned, he had quite enough to keep him busy without adding the Indian Nation to his ever-growing list.

As the young family sat round the fire late one evening, tired, and with another day over and done, there came a knock on the door. Rising reluctantly, for even a willing mind can be weary, the doctor opened the door in preparation for admitting this latest patient.

He always hung a lantern on the porch. The reason for this was twofold. By its light he could more readily identify a caller, read the situation, and perhaps take early cognizance for himself of whatever ailment had brought them in the first place. But another reason moved him to take up this practice. No other home had a lantern burning throughout the night, and by this simple act of consideration, the doctor's home was always easily identifiable to those who may have good reason to find him as quickly as possible. It was always a ready answer to any anxious enquirer of the doctor's whereabouts, *"the cabin with the lantern".*

As the door swung back the young man was not prepared for what he saw. Four men stood on the stoop[6]. It was obvious that three of them were Indians, but the fourth had a mixture of clothing that identified him as an army scout, as did the pistol holstered on his belt. It was the scout that did the talking. In reasonable English he said that a large band of Lakota had come down from the north on an autumn hunting trip, and in the heat of the chase a pony had stumbled and one of their youngest had been trampled by the running herd. They had taken him by pony-drag[7] to the nearest friendly tribe, Cheyenne, and there he lay gravely ill. Could the doctor come?

Dr Carson knew that this could not be an ordinary accident involving a man on a hunt. Death by accident, violence, and disease was a commonplace everyday occurrence among the Indians, there must be something more to tell!

The involvement of the scout also spoke of a deeper interpretation. The scout, of the Crow tribe, was drawing US Army wages, and was taking a big chance by this association with these Indians, and at night time too. However, the porch was not the place to find these answers, and so, after a quick look around, the young doctor beckoned them in.

Apparently, the injured boy was the son of the Sioux chief Gall. He was 18 years old, the chief's last born to his now-dead first wife. The chief had not wished him to go on the hunt, but the others persuaded him, and now his son lay dying two hours away in a Cheyenne camp, stretched along the Rosebud[8]. As the doctor listened to all this, he shook his head slowly. It was too late to travel, and to go with a strange group on such a mission was beyond reasonable expectation. He told them of his concerns, and if they waited till morning, he would go with them. They were insistent however, and the three now entered into a heated exchange with the scout, till at last one of them reached a small piece of paper to the doctor who took it slowly from his hand. The doctor paled as he read it, and took long moments to come to terms with what the scrap of paper had to say. At last he turned to his wife and asked her to make ready his travel bag. He was safe enough to go he said, but he would tell her later of the details.

The Indians could hardly have failed to notice the wide-eyed and wondering child who stood behind his mother's skirt and took in every word. Their buckskins and feathers, their moccasins and beaded breastwork on their tunics and waistcoats, and their weapons too, held the child spellbound. Four such strangers in the confines of their small cabin would without a doubt register deeply on a tender and innocent mind and heart, and images such as this would remain with him for the remainder of his life.

Leaving his wife to do the best she could till he returned, the doctor left immediately in the buggy, carrying splints and such bandages and medicines as he thought he might need. As it turned out, the injured boy had none of the expected *'trample'* injuries common to those who are caught in stampedes, usually internal and fatal. He had been badly bruised though, and had a deep gash across his scalp, resulting in a concussion, but he would live. The doctor, after washing and suturing the wound, stayed for two days till the boy recovered consciousness, and satisfied himself there was no lasting injury. Little did he know that those two days would shape the remainder of his life, and that of his young son too.

It was this incident that spread like a prairie fire throughout the Indian Nation, resulting in Dr Carson's acceptance and respect among the tribes. In all the years he travelled among them, he was never threatened or harmed, and became a frequent visitor to various camps in the years thereafter.

For the next six years the Carson's only child usually accompanied his father on these visits, and his wife too on many occasions, and because the tribe moved frequently to follow the buffalo herds, it meant that very often they were at a distance, and this involved staying overnight.

It was in these years that a bond formed between Carson and a young Indian boy of around the same age, Great Elk, an Arapaho boy. On his visits, the boy and Great Elk would hunt and fish together, and the inherent survival and hunting skills of the Indian ways were little by little imbibed by the white boy.

Their different colours and customs were never a barrier between them; indeed, they seldom noticed them. They were of one mind as far as the great outdoors was concerned, and like all children sometimes fell afoul of childish carelessness. On one occasion they were hunting 'possum and had treed one,[9] the rangy camp dogs barking and howling at the foot of the tree like animals possessed.

Not wishing to leave without the meat, and evening coming on, the boys tried to bring it down with the bow Great Elk carried. The third arrow found its mark, but, piercing right through, prevented the animal from falling! It was lost to them therefore unless they climbed for it, and Great Elk very quickly resolved to do so.

It was coming down again, excited and elated with the kill, that caused him to be careless, and put a foot on a dead branch. The fall was not from a great height, but Great Elk received a deep gash across his forehead, and he felt the sudden stab of pain as his right leg gave way under him. The fall had broken the bone above his ankle. It was a nasty break, and Carson had to run back to the camp for help to get him home. The doctor set the break as best he could, and gave strict instructions as to the care needed in the weeks to come.

However, since the gash on his forehead was a jagged tear, it was impossible to draw the skin cleanly together, (the doctor reckoned he had left a good portion of it on the tree) and this would result in Great Elk being left with a very evident scar that would become more pronounced as he grew older.

Not all their escapades however had such unfortunate endings. On one such outing together Great Elk produced a porcupine quill and, taking Carson's right hand, punctured the ball of his thumb. As the blood began to ooze, he did the same with his own right thumb and then pressed both thumbs together.

In his broken English he then said, *"blood brothers, blood brothers"*. Carson was somewhat taken aback by this, spoken so readily and earnestly, but he gave his hand to his friend, and ever after, when they met, the proffered thumbs pressed together became their very own secret sign of their allegiance to one another.

It was an idyllic relationship the boys had, innocent as only children's relationships can be, and as open and free as the great prairie on which they played and sported together.

Although there were those within the settler community who looked unfavourably on the doctors' Indian visits, yet because they needed his services, they held their counsel on the matter, and it was a source of great and genuine sorrow to all when the news spread that the Carson's had been tragically killed.

Returning one afternoon from a distant camp, a mountain lion spooked their horse, and in the mad and frenzied gallop that followed the buggy overturned, killing both on a rock-strewn section of the trail. The boy was thrown clear and survived, and was found by an Indian hunting party a few hours later. Since they were still several hours from the doctors' cabin, the badly injured child was taken to a couple who lived nearby, Methodist missionaries, and, frontier life being what it was, he remained with them till he was a grown man.

The buggy incident however had caused a deep trauma, and throughout his early teens, Carson could not remember his name, nor even a clear picture of his father and mother. Thus he was known simply as Carson. It was the family name of his parents the missionaries said.

## CHAPTER 4

In time Carson grew to love his new guardians, and they became his parents in his mind and heart. Zack and Grandma Turner were extremely kind to him and treated him like the son they were not able to have. Why they called her grandma when she had no children, he never quite found out. But he finally decided it must have been because she *looked* like a grandma!

A large jolly woman, her broad smile framed by greying wisps of unruly hair, she lavished love and affection on her new arrival. There was no place Carson felt safer than when drawn to her bosom and hugged tightly, and the sweet smells of the scented lye soap from off her skin, and fresh bread aroma coming off her apron, would be something that would remain with him throughout his life.

Grandma Turner was a good cook, and Carson often remembered with nostalgic longing the hotpots, savoury stews and nutritious broths and gravies, and the delicious, new baked bread or cornpone[10] to mop up the last morsel. Sometimes there was not much to work with, for they were not rich people, and there were a few times when scratchings only prevailed in the kitchen, but Grandma Turner could fix even a possum dish like no one else he knew, and nothing was wasted. As he grew older, he would skin and dress whatever meat was for dinner. He always made ready the chitlins[11] for her, and he never tired of watching her prepare the evening meal.

As she sat before the fire, her ingredients beside her, how carefully and unhurriedly she made ready the greens, adding them to the meat pot already simmering on the stove. She was a woman content, and her activity around the cabin reflected that contentment every day. Although a preacher's wife, Grandma Turner never preached at Carson. She had a better way of reaching him.

Never a meal was eaten without a sincere and heartfelt prayer to the Lord for providing it. Every evening, the large brass-bound Bible that always sat upon the table was opened, and from its pages Carson was taught the basics of the Christian Faith. He already remembered some of it from his early childhood, snatches and some stories, and struggled to remember more, so Grandma Turner was gentle with him on that account. Beginning with the Creation, she then taught him of the Great Flood and the reason God sent it.

She did not forget to mention the Lord's dealings with the Jewish people and showed how Jesus, like Moses, when he intervened to save his people, was rejected, and eventually crucified. By Grandma Turner's careful choice of interesting subjects, Carson was led to see the loving nature of God, and gradually, as he grew older, a moral awareness and a responsibility towards God and his fellow man became instilled in him. Not by force, but by the example and sometimes tearful sincerity of Grandma Turner.

When she reached the New Testament, Christ's one and only Sacrifice was impressed firmly on his young heart and mind, and the personal necessity of receiving it for himself. The story of Nicodemus in John chapter three was held up as a warning to all those who would trust only in empty religion for Heaven.

Carson did not at first understand about being Born Again, and felt put out by his inability to grasp it, but Grandma Turner told him it was alright, for Nicodemus did not understand it either, but when Jesus explained it to him, then he understood. This mollified the lad somewhat, for he wouldn't want ever to disappoint Grandma Turner.

Carson had thought it strange when he first saw tears in Grandma
Turner's eyes. She was not one for tears or crying, for all day long she
was a jolly, happy woman. But when it came to explaining the utter
necessity of his salvation, she very often shed tears. This perplexed
him somewhat, but by and by Carson came to understand she was
weeping *for him,* and that realisation only made him love her the
more, and seek to help her when and where he could in the chores
round the cabin.

In the quiet, night time privacy of the little cabin, those scenes had a
profound effect on the lad, for as he laid him down to sleep, he did
so with Grandma Turners tears before him. Carson loved Grandma
Turner, and her evident concern for his soul deeply affected him.

Nothing was forced in his religious upbringing, for Grandma Turner
knew that the Kingdom of Heaven was not achieved without the
Holy Spirit first moving in the heart of the penitent, and she was wise
enough to wait.

Carson learned a lot from Grandma Turner, and moreover, he never
forgot it! It came as no surprise to them therefore when Carson, still
in his teens, committed his life to faith in Christ. His later somewhat
nomadic frontier life did not lend itself to regular religious attendances
and observances, but Carson knew that the whole life of Nicodemus
was filled with such, and they were of no advantage to him when he
sought the kingdom of heaven!

This thought led him to see for himself that although some otherwise
good people sometimes put great store by outward religious
observances, and looked down on him for his apparent neglect of
them, he was not perturbed at this. If those things couldn't save
Nicodemus, he felt he was at no loss without them. The Bible gave

Faith alone as having true value, and if that currency was acceptable to Jesus, then that's the coinage he would use too.

Sometimes folks looked at him oddly if Carson quoted a scripture in his conversations. The West was not accustomed to that, and certainly not from a non-church member, and a ragged and roving frontiersman, but nonetheless, it did not deter him. He loved Grandma Turner and Zack, and they had never pressed him to become either a Methodist or church member, but rather to become a Christian. "Go for that son, aim for that alone and you will not go wrong", old Zack had often repeated.

Moreover, Carson had experienced this entrance of God into his life. The forgiveness of his sins, and the hope of the resurrection. It had happened within him. No one therefore could deny what Carson had within his heart.

Oh, it was not at the mourner's bench at some backwoods revival meeting. There was no ostentatious display of repentance or any other public show. There was no public attendance whatsoever on the day he found his peace. But it was a real event with a time and a place to mark its entrance into his heart, and had thereafter become a living reality every day. He remembered it well.

He had been hunting, and he had been very successful too, but somehow of late he had no satisfaction in the things that usually brought him joy and happiness. This personal unhappiness had blighted every aspect of his life, and it all stemmed from the same source. He was empty and cold toward the things of God, and the joyful faith of old Zack and Grandma constantly in his presence only made his own emptiness more difficult to bear. He had no one near to confide in that day on the prairie, but he suddenly remembered a verse Grandma Turner kept repeating now and again. It was where Jesus said, *"Come unto me all ye that labour and are heavy laden, and I will give you rest. Take my yoke upon you and learn of me."*

Suddenly Carson saw that the burden of his own unworthiness and sinfulness was borne by the Saviour himself at Calvary, and did not Isaiah say, *"Surely he hath borne our griefs and carried our sorrows".* It was that very moment, when the light shone into his soul, that he drew rein on his horse and fell on his knees to the earth confessing, and at the same time accepting, the open invitation of forgiveness the gospel offered.

From that time forward his newfound faith shaped his thinking, guided his decisions, and more than once gave him courage to face certain violent death, from which, in the providence of his Heavenly Father, he had been spared. Why would Carson then be turned aside from such a precious, daily comfort through the slights and judgments of others, or the disdain of any religious establishment, who were often more anxious to convert people to their membership roll than to save their souls? If the Lord *kept saints in Caesar's household,* and He did, then He could keep Carson on the frontier.

# CHAPTER 5

Zack Turner, in contrast to his wife, was a small wiry man with piercing blue eyes and a complexion brown as a nut from long years in the saddle. His missionary duties required him to ride a circuit, which he rode constantly when weather permitted, and even sometimes when it didn't! In character, he was the essence of kindness itself, and that kindness found its expression in a life devoted to his Lord. It was his long absences from home that left Grandma Turner the task of caring for Carson, but when he was at home, he did not neglect his young charge.

Zack had known since the boy came to them that he would require extra care and attention, not only from a physical point of view but also from the social side of things. It soon became clear that the child had been sheltered. There was no doubt about that, and his experience of life outside his early home was limited indeed. Just how limited was exposed one day in the small and rustic hamlet they called a township.

Zack had bought the lad a pony, and any riding he needed to do apart from his circuit duties, he always took the lad with him. It was good for the boy to get away from the confines of the cabin, and Zack looked at this as a means of expanding the boy's knowledge of everyday life and experiencing needful interaction with others besides him and Grandma Turner. It was on one such outing that an incident occurred that left Zack in no doubt of the task he had before him if he was to teach the boy of the outside world.

Leaving the boy to tend the horses while he made a quick purchase, Zack returned to a very excited and wondering child.

"Zack, Zack, I have just seen a man who was black all over. He was with a wagon passing through and he was walking with the oxen, driving them on. What happened to him Zack, was he sick?" For a brief moment, Zack was tempted to laugh heartily at the innocent naivety and excitement in the child's face, but he checked himself just in time. It would never do to stifle the lad's enquiring nature, or to offend him by being amused at his open, guileless manner. "Are you telling me son that you ain't never seen a nigger[12] before?" "What's a nigger Zack," the boy asked earnestly.

"Just exactly what you saw son, a black person." "Where do they come from Zack, are they from these parts", the young Carson continued, clearly absorbed now with this discovery. "Well, their original homeland would be Africa most likely, but there are thousands of them here now working the plantations of the Southern states."

"Why do they come over here Zack, are they settlers like us?" "No, not exactly lad, far from it. They are stolen from their land, kidnapped, men, women, and children too, and brought over here on slave ships and made to work like mules and burros.[13] They fetch big money too in the markets."

"Aw, come on Zack, you're joshin' me. You can't buy people."

"I wish I was joshin' you boy, but it's all too true. I have seen them myself, standing on a market stool and being examined like animals. Teeth examined like you would a horse, feet and legs too. Some of them made to walk just to make sure they aren't lame. Beaten if they don't walk fast enough. I tell you son it was not a pretty sight. I saw children torn brutally from their mother's arms, never to see each other again. The wails and screams of those people received no mercy from the buyers. Pretty young girls greedily bid upon by evil old men. I tell you there will come a day of reckoning for what I saw happening to those niggers. No civilised country could prosper for long with such cruel and unrighteous deeds allowed to continue among them."

The lad was visibly taken aback by Zack's words. Shocked and silenced by the revelation just made to him. Zack was serious, Carson thought, and Zack could tell the boy was trying to process all this and finding it difficult. As no more questions were coming, Zack put his arm around the silent and perplexed young lad.

"Son, this world is not all that it appears to be sometimes, and people are not all they appear to be either. If we are happy in life and our circumstances, we ought to thank the Almighty for that, but we ought never to forget that the whole creation is under the curse of old Adam's sin. *Thorns and thistles* from the earth, and *wars and bloodshed* among the nations are the lot of mankind. We cannot change it, but it is always wise to know it and be aware of it.

Best thing is to be just and equal to all, and treat others as we ourselves would like to be treated. If others do evil, they must and will give account for themselves when that great day of judgement finally appears. Just rest in that son, and trust in the good Lord for those things you don't understand. Never allow the sins of others to turn you from the path of righteousness.

We can seldom change what our rulers do when they get into power, so it is always wise to know what a man believes before we vote for them!" Laying a hand on the boy's shoulder Zack said, "Let's go get Grandma Turner some eggs if we can find them, and maybe a stick of candy for yourself. There ain't no law says eatin' candy is a sin."

Thus it was, little by little, that the young Carson was brought to a knowledge of the practicalities of life. By his kind attention old Zack made sure that the child was made aware of life's dangers and pitfalls, and in time to become independent, and confident within himself of the life choices and decisions he would make. It was indeed the happiest of unions. Zack and the boy lived in the ever-present joy of true companionship, and Zack often had cause to thank the Lord that the Indian hunting party were led to his door, and not someone else's!

The winter months were spent mostly in Zack's study, which was also his workshop, repairing harness, making knives or tools, cleaning his weapons, or pouring lead bullets and making patches for them. In those times how the boy listened as Zack both showed and demonstrated the care needed to maintain any flintlock[14] in good working order. In the soft lamp glow of the little room, he watched spellbound as the old man demonstrated the skills needed for frontier life.

Beginning with the firing and trigger mechanism, Zack carefully first cleaned and then wiped each part, including where the flint struck the frizzen.[15] The hammer and mainspring were checked with care, and a little grease was added with the point of a goose quill if needed. The piece of flint held in the screw-lock jaws atop the hammer was carefully reseated and tightened again in place. The importance of frizzen and pan[16] was carefully explained to the wondering boy standing taking all this in. If the spark does not get to the powder in the pan, or if the powder in the pan becomes caked through dampness, all was lost as far as a successful shot was concerned. Since gunpowder naturally drew the damp, these things therefore needed particular attention.

Zack pointed out something that very many men in their haste forgot. The tiny touchhole or vent, that allowed the powder in the pan, when ignited, to travel inside the breech to the main charge, was a crucial part that required careful cleaning regularly. If a touchhole becomes blocked by dirt, or caked with damp powder, all the shooter gets is a 'flash in the pan,'[17] or worse, a hang fire'[18] and the opportunity is lost for either hunting or defensive protection.

The young Carson often watched as Zack took particular care in rounding off each lead ball as it fell from the mould into the cooling pan. Making sure it was smooth and uniform, and that each patch was likewise shaped with care. This, Zack told Carson, was to ensure that with each powder load, itself measured and poured with care, the results would always be the same. It was good advice, and many years later Carson followed the same in his own preparation, before progress brought the brass bound cartridge and breech-loading rifle.

Unlike many preachers, Zack Turner carried a rifle. It was a Kentucky long rifle, and he had a pistol to match. He often said that the kindness of his Christianity was not to be taken as cowardice. He had a very simple philosophy in this regard, which he was only too willing to explain to those who questioned the armaments he carried, *"if the good Lord gives us good things, the least we can do to show our appreciation is to defend them"!*

On his travels, as well as his riding mount, Zack led a pack mule. He had several reasons for this. It gave him a wider scope in his work and enabled him to reach settlements and cabins of more than a day's ride, for he could make camp on the trail if needs be. He could also carry his gospel pamphlets and tracts, and, as providence supplied, Bibles. The other reason was more domestic.

Zack rarely came home empty-handed as far as game was concerned, and he could throw a couple of bucks across the mule, and maybe a few prairie chickens and a turkey or two as well. Game was plentiful if one knew where to look, and on his return journeys, if the weather was warm, rather than risk the meat spoiling, he would wait till he got within half a day's ride from home, and he would hunt from there homeward.

Sometimes he could not use all he shot of course, especially in warmer weather, but he had an agreement with a local settler who had a large family, and who was glad of the meat in exchange for ploughing and preparing Grandma Turner's little garden. Once ploughed, and well fertilised with buffalo[19] chips that local youngsters brought her, Grandma Turner could break up what she needed and sow her vegetables and squashes.[20]

Her garden was a talking point among the settlers around, and in a good year, Grandma Turner could trade off some of her produce for more labour-intensive crops, like maize or potatoes, so it was a very useful arrangement for all parties. Thus Zack's hunting led, in a roundabout way, to the ongoing provision of the cabin's needs, and it did Zack good to be able to contribute thus, for his long absences from home responsibilities sometimes were a heavy burden on his conscience.

For his hunting, Zack used a .40 Calibre rifle. He could have used a larger bore, but larger bores meant more lead and more powder, and he had confidence that the calibre he used could bring down anything he could throw across the saddle, and that was his marker. He could manage a buck, but anything larger he would leave for someone else.

His pistol was of the same calibre, which meant his lead slugs and patches were compatible with both weapons, and this saved a great inconvenience when on the trail.

# CHAPTER 6

It was one such evening in the cabin workshop, as he had just finished mending the stock of an old rifle, Zack turned to the lad with the words, "Try that lad, see how it comes up to your eye." Carson reached for the gun and smoothly brought it to aim. In one practised movement, he had it snug into his shoulder and firm to the touch, with his eye running naturally along the barrel. There was no squinting, or trying to find the front sight as is very often the case with beginners. Zack smiled. Carson had done this before of course, and he did not forget the lessons learned. He had proved himself a worthy student.

Putting a loving hand on the boy's shoulder Zack then said, "tomorrow we are going hunting. You have come of age and I have some things to say that I want you to consider and learn. Ponder well what I tell you tomorrow, for it will be to your advantage throughout your life. In the morning, I want you to saddle the two riding horses, I will tend to the mule myself. Have them ready for sun up, for right after breakfast we are leaving.

Little did the boy know just how far-reaching tomorrow would be, and how prophetic old Zack's words would prove to be. As he closed his eyes to sleep he did so with Zack's words filling his mind and thoughts.

As the pair rode out next morning it was indeed a pristine winter scene. The light snow, the first that had fallen, had already frozen, made for easy riding, and the rising sun, glinting brightly through the trees, made for a happy prospect indeed for the two friends.

Not much was said on the outgoing trail, for the beauty of the morning held both in its spell, and they just gave themselves to the experience from hearts that were thankful to be alive. After about an hour Zack reigned in and dismounted, beckoning Carson to follow. He led his mount through a stand of timber, until the view opened up into a wide and secluded clearing. Tying his horse securely, he then proceeded to unload the mule. Drawing out a rifle from a deerskin scabbard, and bringing a powder horn and shot, he walked to where Carson was just finishing with his mount.

"I have something for you," he said. "Grandma and I have decided it is time for you to learn a few things. You have grown big enough, and we know you are wise enough to trust, so now's the time to begin." As he spoke these words, he handed him the rifle and hung the horn over his shoulder. "It's yours son, and it's a good one. We bought it from an old trapper's widow, but he always said he would like it to go to someone who would appreciate it, and care for it like he did."

As Carson took the rifle he did so in silence. The very joy of handling such a weapon was enough to stir and gladden any man's heart, let alone a teenage boy, but to be given it as a present was something else again. Carson would never forget this moment in time, as the full implications of Zack's words began to sink in.

The rifle was favoured on the frontier among hunters and trappers. A Hawken .40 calibre, its Curly Maple[21] buttstock and fore piece ran the length of the rifle, and was beautifully fashioned and polished till it shone with a deep, dull gleam. The brass patch box[22] in the buttstock stood out richly against the dark wood stain the maker had used, and the eyelets of the ramrod matched the patch box in quality and beauty.

Carson was thrilled, he could hardly believe this was happening to him, as he ran a hand up and down its graceful length as if to be sure it was really true! "Oh Zack, how can I thank you and Grandma for this" he cried, his voice breaking with hardly suppressed emotion. "Just use it wisely and well son, and that will be our satisfaction and joy in giving it, but right now let's see what you can do with it."

Taking a piece of old trapper cured[23] deer hide, with a charcoal mark in the middle the size of a silver dollar, he reached it to Carson. "Take that and fix it to yonder deadfall and come back here".

When the lad returned Zack bade him first load his rifle, then prime it. That target is 100 yards away son, and I want you to zero your piece on it. The rifle is zeroed already at around a hundred yards or so, for I tried it, but every man finds his own zero, for every man shoulders a rifle differently. Individual zero is very important for accurate shooting, exact shot placement, as opposed to hitting the general chest kill zone, which is the size of a skillet, but shot placement is what I want you to learn today. Anyone can hit a deer, but killing it cleanly with a well-placed shot is another matter entirely.

Lean your shoulder against this tree here, and your right elbow in the fork of the branch. Good balance and rifle rest are always important, and you have it today so you might as well use it. Now rest your left arm along the branch, as suits you, with the fore end of the rifle in the palm of your hand, lying easily, fingers holding it lightly but firmly. You want the recoil to come straight back. If you strangle the fore-end by holding too tightly the rifle will jump, and you want to avoid that.

Remember you are going for a tight cluster of strikes here, once we see you are hitting consistently then we can bring the cluster to the dead centre later.

"Ok, now have a go. Take your time, take a deep breath, concentrate on your sights, keeping them on the target as you are slowly breathing out and squeezing on the trigger. The shot should come as a surprise to you".

Carson took up his firing position, his mind trying to keep all Zacks instructions as he did so. Taking careful aim while breathing out gently, he applied gentle pressure, and suddenly the sear[24] released. There had been no creep,[25] no travel in the trigger mechanism, and the suddenness took him by surprise. But the crack of the shot, that familiar and comforting sound, brought all his former tension to an end.

Zack said, "Now do it again, twice more, and remember to aim exactly where you did the first time".

At the third shot, Zack sent the young Carson for the target and watched with some amusement as he studied the strikes on his way back.

"Well, how did you do son", the old man enquired, and Carson reached the piece of deerskin to him without a word.

A silver dollar is not big at a hundred yards, but three neat round holes formed a little group to the left of centre, all just edging on the charcoal mark. Turning to Carson Zack said, "That inch to the left could be your particular style, your hold on the rifle, or it could be the sights need a little nudge to correct it. Either way son, I am very proud of you. It's a long time since I have seen a match of that, not in a coon's age. Keep in mind now what you have done here this morning. Soon you will learn for yourself to compensate for windage,[26] or to use a holdover[27] on a longer shot to take account of bullet drop. But right now, we will go and see if you can get Grandma Turner some venison."

# CHAPTER 7

nother hour up the trail Zack again reined in and dismounted. In a low voice he said, "I have known of this place for a long time, and each time I came I never failed to see game. Let's be very quiet and see what today brings." Tying their mounts a little off the trail they made their way on foot for a couple of hundred yards, taking care in the placing of each step, and making sure that nothing they carried made a sound either. As the trees thinned out Zack crept even slower, till he came to a place where an old stump provided a seat to the view beyond.

Sure enough, their caution paid off. Out in a grassy clearing a small herd of around a dozen Whitetails grazed peacefully. They were scattered. The furthest out was 200 yards or so, but three were well within range for Zack's purpose that day. Carson's rifle was already loaded and primed, but Zack bade the boy rest his rifle and wait, beckoning with his hand for him to sit a spell.

Finally Zack spoke, looking earnestly at the boy beside him. "Son, Grandma and I don't have much to give you by way of education or position in society. We are poor people, as I am sure you have already noticed. Not only are we not educated ourselves, but we cannot afford to send you back East to college. We have spoken long on your future for all that, and are desirous that we do our best for you till you come to the age of making up your own mind as to what you want to do. We have decided therefore that whatever we *don't* have, ought not to hinder us from using what we *do* have. That is my intention today. To use what I have, to share what I can, in the hope that it will give you a skill worthy of the name.

This is the frontier lad. Life is hard out here. Go to many a settler's cabin and see what they have. Oh, they may have laid claim to their section, and have their markers down, but what do they have by way of life's necessities and provisions? Dirt farmers, that's what they are, and poor dirt farmers at that.

Scrabbling a living from soil that would sooner sprout thorns and cactus as wheat or rye. Hard, backbreaking work day after day. Scratching a daily living in the hope that somehow their offspring will have it better than they had! Their wives and children need no comment as to their poverty, they are themselves a living commentary on poverty! Ragged in summer and cold in winter. Clothed in the livery of destitution, not being able to read and write, barefoot, and hungry most of the time, they cannot fail to arouse pity within a human breast. Moreover, if and when such pioneers do reach a point where things improve for them, they are too old or too crippled with ill health to enjoy it. On my travels, I see this, and it never fails to touch my heart in fellow feeling for them.

Grandma and I don't want that for you son. You may never be rich, we are not concerned about that, for riches have their snares, but we want you to be able to provide, not only for your own needs, but for the needs of any family you may have. It is with this in mind that I have brought you out here today. Before anyone can be anything in this life, and more so here on the frontier, they must live, they must survive, they must get by every day. This being so it brings the issue very clearly to this, they must eat!

I can teach you how to survive son. How to get by, how to eat as it were, until you find your own calling in life, whatever that may be. Are we on the same trail son? Can you follow my sign? Are we still riding together?"

"Sure Zack, sure. I am with you. I understand well what you've told me. When you were telling of the dirt farmer's children, I even had a picture of the Monroe's in my mind. You know them, Zack. They live a few miles up the creek from us, and I even thought you were describing them".

"Yes son, I know them, mores the pity, but the frontier has thousands just like the Monroe's, and it was the thousands I had in mind".

Zack shifted his seat on the stump and made himself more comfortable, keeping his eyes on the grazing deer as he did so. Then he looked again at the boy beside him and after a moment to collect his thoughts he began.

"You have always shown a great interest in any game I ever brought home. As a matter of fact you have been a very useful pair of hands in the preparation of it, and many a time I said to Grandma, that lad is a natural. He can skin a buck and bone it out as good as I can. Many a time I said those very words, son. Indeed, it was your willingness and ability that gave us the idea in the first place.

There is always a market here on the frontier for fresh meat. People are moving west all the time, and they will be your customers. Whether it be miners, settlers, passing immigrants on the wagon trains, the army, or even supplying a small township, fresh meat, well-dressed and presented, has an attraction all its own. If you know your trade you will never be short of a dollar if you can provide it. The outlay will be minimal. A good horse and a pack mule or two, and your rifle. All you need then is the skill and patience to go after it. Out here even fur is valuable, so nothing is wasted. Meat can also be traded for any other necessities you might need. Between cash and barter you need never want son.

Today I am going to show you the basics of hunting for meat, and not for sport. You might not follow it for your life calling, but you will always have it, and having it will be like money in the bank, it will be there when you need it! It is an honourable profession, not everyone can do it well, and you will be your own master.

Now, see those animals out there before us, they are representative of all that you will be hunting for the table. Bear, caribou, deer, elk, or moose. Even for the big shaggies the same principles apply, for buffalo too must be pursued with a hunter's instinct. I want you to be the best there is at what you do, and beginning young is a head start not every man gets the chance at. Of course, there are a thousand other things you will and must learn as you travel this road, but they will come in time, and many of them will come from your observations, but the successful kill is where it all begins. You have already gotten close to your target through silence and keeping out of sight, rule number one, now is the time to make your choice of beast, the distance to it, and the shot.

See how those animals out there continually lift their heads, all at random times, each taking note of what is happening around them. If we were closer, we could see their ears and noses are continually moving and twitching, catching the wind, and every little sound that is made. Their eyesight also is very sharp, so always keep that in mind too. Once you allow either sight, sound or smell to come from you, your chance is gone. And you needn't wait around, they will not come back!

No quick movements, no noise, keep always downwind, and you are in with a chance of taking home dinner. I prefer windy weather for my hunting, and for three good reasons. If the wind is blowing and it's in your favour, then you are safe from the little changes that often happen in still weather, when for some reason an unseen little shift in the air allows your scent to be carried to your target. Also, in windy weather tiny noises are masked and, best of all, when the foliage is constantly moving, any small movements of your own will go unnoticed.

In picking your target pick a single beast, and don't be distracted by the others around it. Choose one without others close beyond it. You don't want to wound another animal if you miss your intended one. Note first if it is walking steadily and evenly, and that it is not limping or sickly. You want a healthy animal, not what's left of someone else's bad shooting.

Try and take a broadside shot, but if it must be a frontal shot wait till it lifts its head, and place your shot anywhere up the centre of the neck, or, if you prefer, at the base of the neck, right where it meets the breastbone. Plumb centre there leads straight to the heart. I once took this shot but was just a little to the left. I got my beast but it ran 200 yards and I had to track it to find it. Try and centre if possible. Dead centre.

Keep sight of your target at the shot. You will see it either jump or stagger, but it will react, that's for sure. It might even run a little, but will rapidly show signs of bleeding - out, finally falling. Likewise, if you miss you will know also. It will perhaps stand at the alert, head held high, watching. If this is the case it will be readily recognisable to you. Keep in mind too that a chest-shot animal will bleed - out inwardly, but a headshot beast will need to be bled, either from piercing the heart or cutting its throat. I always bleed my kills. It makes for better meat and leaves the cooking preparation less messy.

Something else. If you are fortunate enough to have a firing point well hidden from the animal, and where they cannot see the flash from the pan, or you reloading, you might even get another shot while they try and make up their minds where the shot is coming from. If they cannot see you, they are often inquisitive enough to stand and observe before finally bolting off. Those that fall beside them seem to hold no alarm for them.

I once shot three one morning by that very method, so keeping out of sight is very important if at all possible. Now son, bearing in mind what I have just said, can you single out a target and try the Hawken?"

As Carson marked his chosen animal, Zack spoke again in low tones. "A chest shot is always a winner, but I have my favourite shot when circumstances are right for it, want to try it?" The lad nodded eagerly as he kept the rifle on the beast he had singled out, a fine buck, sleek and fat. Right then lad, follow a line behind his foreleg right up to the shoulder till about four inches from the top, the breadth of your hand only, and squeeze the trigger gently. Keep particular sight of him all the while, concentrate on that, and don't allow the flash or the recoil to distract you, and to make you lose sight of him. I want you to see the strike if you can. There is no hurry. Take your time. All the advantage is yours at this very moment, make it count. Hardly daring to breathe, Carson slowly but surely followed the procedure that had given him such success on the old deerskin target that morning.

He trusted Zack, and he wanted to please him, but he also wanted to claim a first kill with his new rifle. Suddenly the Hawken punched back into his shoulder, the smoke from the muzzle forming a whitish-blue haze that blotted out the scene momentarily, but not before he saw the results of Zack's quiet advice. The animal's legs just folded under it and it fell on the spot, motionless. It was an image that would not be easily forgotten by the boy, nor would the intense relief that flowed over him as he surveyed the distant kill, *his kill,* now just a buff-coloured smudge against the green of the meadow.

Zack's hand gently rested on his shoulder, and the low voice came again to his ear. "You have done well today son, and before we leave, I will show you why I asked you to take that particular shot, and your kill will demonstrate just how effective it is."

Walking to the fallen animal Zack continued his narrative to his young charge. "I am going to do this myself son, for you must do it yourself when the situation arises, I want you to watch carefully all I do here, and you will know the details of the simple yet very important first procedure of processing a fresh kill to the best advantage. In warm weather the sooner it is done the better to avoid bloating, in fact do it immediately, for opening the beast allows it to cool as quickly as possible".

Coming from behind the animal Zack first prodded it vigorously with the toe of his boot. "Never underestimate a big animal son, always make sure it is dead, the last thing you want is an antler or horn tearing you open. It only takes seconds to check, so make sure it is dead."

Zack then turned the animal on its back and held it there between his feet while he cut a neat line from the groin to the breast bone, but through the hide only, Carson noted he did not cut into the stomach cavity.

Then, turning the knife edge upwards, he held it by the blade, with the tip of his forefinger just below the knife point. Making a tiny hole at the groin through to the cavity, he now entered his forefinger and blade point. It was easy now to run the knife the length of the slit hide, while his fingertip below the knife point made sure that neither stomach nor intestine was cut or punctured. "We don't want the meat to be contaminated by the gut contents son, nor will your buyer, so keep that little tip in mind".

Carson watched in silent wonderment as the old man busied himself effortlessly at the animal, and noted how, with apparent ease, it all came so naturally to him.

Allowing the beast to fall again on its flank, Zack pulled the cavity opening a little wider and the stomach suddenly ballooned out on the grass, followed by the entrails. It appeared huge in relation to the animal Carson thought, and as he was thinking so Zack quickly finished his task. Reaching into the cavity with his left hand he first gathered together the connecting vessels that held the stomach attached, and then carefully brought the knife blade to beyond his closed left fist, and, working blind, deftly cut them, allowing the complete removal of the whole digestive system. He would remove the liver later. Not every man follows my procedure son, but I am always careful with this part, and I have good reasons to be. It is clean, complete, and I still have all my fingers! Straightening up, Zack pointed with his knife at the stomach and entrails on the ground.

"There's easily 30 pounds dead weight lying there, and a buck is easier thrown over the saddle without that. Here, grab hold of an antler and we'll get back and get a fire going".

The coffee pot lid began to lift with the pressure from within and Zack leaned forward to remove it from the coals. They had taken a break before they returned home. Grandma Turner had wrapped some cornbread in a cloth and, with a small jar of salt and some butter, had placed all in a basket with some homemade lemonade and biscuit. It was plain fare, but with what Zack had planned was just what they needed.

They had already hung the deer on a low branch beside them and had now removed the remaining innards. Liver, heart, lungs and kidneys. These he carefully laid aside on a clean patch of grass. After Zack had opened up the cavity with a short stick across the rib line to allow the carcass to cool, with his knife he whittled and sharpened a few skewers, and loaded them with bite-sized pieces from his grass patch larder. Holding the loaded skewers over the reddened coals, he slowly turned his until the meat was to his liking, and watched as the boy did the same.

"This is a feast fit for a king," old Zack said with a laugh, and Carson was not about to differ. He was hungry, and as he trickled salt along his now-ready meat he could not believe food could taste so good.

"Son, this is a grand country, and there is abundance for all in it, but remember, it is for use and not abuse. There was a dozen or more deer in that meadow, but we only needed one. Always remember, only to take what you can use, or what some other little family can use."

Nodding to the carcass, Zack continued. "From the tongue to the tail, that animal has more usable and nourishing provision than most folk from back East could ever imagine. Even here on the frontier, many never utilise all that is found there. They invariably think of the haunches, the shoulders, and the loin, but what about the head, the neck, the chitlins, and what we have just eaten? Some men skin their kill where it falls, using its hide to keep the meat clean and off the ground, and then only remove the quarters. In doing so they leave as much behind them for the coyotes and buzzards as would feed a small family for a week.

You'd be surprised just how much meat remains after quartering. But if you take the ribs and backbone with you, and with an axe chop into short lengths, just to fit in your pot, a few hours over a slow fire will repay any effort or time you have taken. You have not yet eaten the head meat, but you will, and you will like it too.

It can be cooked in two ways. By skinning and boiling it with the ribs and bones, or by burning off[28] the fur over the hot coals, scraping it clean to the skin, and boiling it with the skin on. Just drop it into a pot and let it simmer, the longer the better. Then remove it, let it cool, and the meat will come off by fingertip. Cut in small pieces and dab it in a little salt, and you have a supper. I tell you son if you never had worse than that you would never go hungry.

You remember the Donner Party[29] that were trapped in the Sierra Nevada a couple of years ago. It was the talk of the frontier. Over eighty people set out, and only half made it. The living ate the dead to survive. It was an ill-conceived trip from the very beginning, but it was not the only time people were caught out through carelessness.

Long before you were born, we had a similar experience that all but wiped us out but for the Grace of the Almighty.

I was just a child then, but old enough to take in what was happening, and old enough to remember the fear that I felt during those days in our little cabin.

All those who had come west for a great adventure, trappers, settlers, miners and dudes, got an awakening that winter all right. When the spring thaw came many were found dead in their cabins. Frozen in their beds. They had no food, no water, no firewood, and the cold had claimed them where they lay.

But for the foresight Pa had, we would have been lost too. Not far from where we had settled at that time was a camp of Arapaho and Cheyenne, along with some Sioux. It was a mixed bunch, but they did not bother us and we did not bother them. Pa always said that "Us kids could learn a lot from them injun's, for those that could survive in 'hide tents' as he called them, with only buffalo and berries to eat, must be right smart people." That's what Pa always said.

It was that same fall that Pa took his own advice and prepared for a winter that the signs said was coming. On his many journeys to and from a stand of old cottonwoods, where we got our firewood, Pa watched the Indians as they stayed on the river fishing for longer than usual. Smoke racks were everywhere, loaded with fish, and the daily haze of the smoke fires hung over the tepees. The squaws were busy from dawn to dusk, and the fires were kept going throughout the night. The older of the children gathered berries and nuts for the pemmican and could be seen in groups scattered far and wide over the hills and prairie. The young men hunted longer than usual too. When drying and smoking came to an end, and the weather favoured it, fresh meat was hung up out of reach of vermin and critters to freeze in the fur.

Pa saw all this and knew something was in the wind. Us children wondered when he came home one day and began his preparation around the cabin. But we just did as we were told without asking too many questions. Ma knew, but she never said, I suppose not wanting to scare us unnecessarily.

When that blizzard hit that winter, we already had a cord[30] of firewood built on the stoop, right beside our door, and enough river water to last for days already in kegs. Pa had a young buck hanging close alongside the firewood, and we never saw daylight for eight days till that Norther blew itself out. All that we had above ground was lost. The two mules and our cow froze to death in the barn, and the chickens froze on the roost. We had already killed a hog that fall, and so we were not without hog fat and bacon, and we had the buck. The root cellar[31] kept our greens safe, but the other hog we lost to the cold.

It took us a while to recover from that, but Pa managed and always said it was the Indians that gave him the warning. "Yes Sir", he said ever afterward, "Them Injuns sure know this country, I always told you they were right smart people." Pa was not a religious man back then. Among other things he made corn liquor, for *'medicinal purposes'* he said, but Ma said the 'medicine' he took was far and above the dose he needed! Woe betides us if we crossed him in those times. He was a good man, but set in his ways, and he kept us children at work around the cabin. But after that blizzard he changed. We could see it, and we knew it, and were taught it.

I never forget those times even now, and that's why I am telling you all this. We were afraid for those eight days. Although the stove was kept lit night and day, the cold could still be felt, and the blizzard's howl was continually in our ears. Even Pa was afraid, I suppose mostly for us children, but I saw it in his face and never forgot it. After that he always told us never to be ashamed of being afraid, for fear, rightly understood and handled, is the best friend we can have out here.

Fear will give us eyes to see dangers where others are blind to them. Fear will make us wise to the signs, seasons and times so that we will prepare for them, and don't let them pass neglected. Never take this country for granted son. Always be prepared for the worst, and you will always come off best."

Young Carson hung on Zack's every word. He had not spoken a word since he fired the shot, so enthralled was he with the newness of all the old man had shown him. Zack did not lecture, but told the boy kindly and simply what he knew and had experienced.

He had just proved so with Carson's shot, and now the carcass hung beside them. They had already eaten a tasty meal from what many folks would cast away, and Carson did not doubt in his young mind that all of what Zack said was to be taken as fact, real and true. It had been an unforgettable morning, and he had a lot to remember, but being a witness to it, seeing it done, was as good as having it written down, better even, for he could relive at will any scene he so desired.

Before he doused the fire Zack had one last thing to show the wondering boy. Walking to the carcass he ran his fingers through the hide over the shoulders till he found what he wanted, the strike where the ball had entered and exited. "See that. That ball did not stop in your kill but passed right through. Had another animal been alongside yours that ball would have wounded it. Always avoid that.

Remember I told you to aim high on the shoulder, just four inches down from the top? Here's why. Your shot broke the spine, and that's why the beast fell immediately and lay motionless. There is only one other shot that can accomplish that, and that is a headshot, a brain shot. A heart shot[32] is always fatal needless to say, but I have seen animals run with their heart shattered. Not far it is true, but they did run. Had they been grazing by a riverbank, or on the edge of a mountain path, they may have been lost.

The high shoulder aim has another advantage. It gives you plenty of leeway in lateral movement, and if you are a fraction low and miss the bone, the lungs are just under it, and present a broad, sure target. A lung shot is a very good shot too, but with it your beast will run, not far, maybe 50 or 60 yards at most.

But enough for today. How's about getting back to Grandma Turner and letting her share in our good fortune. Tomorrow is the Lord's Sabbath, and she will want something special for it now that we have it."

# CHAPTER 8

Carson's time with the missionary couple was a blessed one, a happy one, and a big part of him wanted to stay, for as he looked back on his childhood with them, he did so with a sense of fulfilment and satisfaction. There were no dark places in it, and each time his mind turned to his childhood it was always a happy scene that came before him.

He had treasured Zack's company and his never-ending words of wisdom and encouragement, and he dearly loved Grandma Turner, but as he grew older, he knew he had to make his own way in the world. Surrounded as he was by trappers, mountain men, trail guides and prospectors, his father's wanderlust slowly grew in him with an intensity that he could no longer contain.

The Rockies, with their promise of lucrative fur for those brave enough to claim it, beckoned daily. However, unless he was willing to work for a fur company at a set wage, he needed a grubstake to set himself up for his first winter in the mountains. He was not inclined to work under contract, so he decided to work alone and free, beholden to none.

He was nearing twenty-one when he first broached the subject and his plans with the old couple. They never spoke, but knowing looks passed between them now and then until finally, the man who had been his father for so long, rose from the table and led him into the private quarters of the little cabin they had shared as a family. His wife followed slowly.

"We knew this time would come son," he said, "but we waited until it came from you. After the accident that claimed your parents, you were very ill for a month or two. In that time we took it upon ourselves to settle your father's estate, such as it was, selling off the few cattle, his mules and his medical equipment. Had we left it thieves would have carried it away bit by bit.

As you may know the cabin itself was rented from the storekeeper McCallister, but we gathered the furniture together and put it up for auction. We only kept the small, most personal items such as the family Bible, your mother's wedding band and your father's old trunk and contents. As your mother and I cleared out the homestead the old trunk had much to reveal.

Under the assortment of items and papers we found this money belt, and inside a slip of paper which you might like to see." Carson took the paper and read the words so clearly written in ink.

*Jason Carson MD. Departing Plymouth May 30, 1830. Shipbound for the New World.*

Carson lifted his eyes off the paper and looked at the couple who had been his sole living kin here on the frontier. "I never knew," he said, "and it never crossed my mind that my parents must have had possessions to leave behind. Thank you for this, it answers the question of my origin and gives me a point of focus as to my roots, something I never had before. As he turned to leave the room, Zack caught him by the arm, "Wait" he said, "there's more."

Going to a wardrobe he lifted a false floor and drew out a buckskin bag, and a smaller bundle within it. The first was heavy, and as he put it in Carson's hand he said,

"Your father's estate. All of it. All told the sales produced good prices at auction, as people knew it would eventually come to you, and bid accordingly. But on top of that, still within the old money belt, were 50 gold pieces. I assume they came with him from Plymouth. This little bag here however was found when I went to recover the bodies."

Separate from the cash contents and papers of the larger bag was the other bundle that Zack now held to view. It was an old piece of woollen cloth, heavily stained and carrying the grime of years. Greenish in colour, gathered at the corners, and tied with a thin sliver of willow bark. It was heavy too. The old man continued. "I found this in your father's medical bag the very day I retrieved the bodies, and it took me a while to figure it out, but eventually it became clear.

The doctor, your father, never refused those requests the Indians now and then made to him, and they would not be in his debt. They are generous people, and once a trust is built, they both live it and give it.

They knew that the Wasi'cu[33] would not benefit from any of those things the Indians themselves treasured and prized, and so they paid him in what they knew the white man would use. Gold!

These are nuggets, large nuggets, placer [34] gold. River gold. Nuggets not mined, but panned from banks and bars in the river, and by the looks of them found not far from the mother lode. Note they are smooth, no sharp edges like gold chiselled from the rock and separated from the quartz, but not so smooth either as to be in the river very long."

As Carson took all this in, he looked earnestly and perhaps a little questioningly at Zack, and Zack then explained. "I was not always a preacher son. Before I met your mother I panned gold for five years in the Sierras, until my partner got killed in a landslide. I was with him and was injured, but I survived. After that I lost heart and came back to the Dakotas, and it was then that I found the Lord and my present calling. I also found your mother, I mustn't forget that, must I?

I worked for a while in an assay office, and that gave me an appreciation of the subtle but important differences in gold from various origins. I got quite good at it, and it got so that I could tell from the poke[35] a miner brought in where he found it. If his story did not tally with the colour of his gold then it was most likely stolen! We saw plenty of that too.

This is why this bag your father left has taken my interest. This is not Dakota gold, it's the wrong colour, this comes from much further west, from the Sierras. The thing that puzzles me is this. Why would an Indian, living in these parts, have and give such a generous amount of Sierra gold as a present? Can't explain it no how.

Whatever the reason, by doing so these Indians showed their trust in him, that the origin of this 'Indian gold' would never be disclosed to another. As it was, the situation never arose, for he died with the Indian's kindness unopened.

Your father was a temperate man, well respected and trusted, and the same day as I laid him in the grave, I made a promise that I would continue his role in your upbringing. I hope now today that my promise can be said to be fulfilled, for I have delivered your father's inheritance to you son."

Carson was speechless, he would find a means later to honour the love this couple had shown, but in his hands he now held his trapper's grubstake, and much more, and considering its origin and story behind it, he resolved there and then to honour all his benefactors in using it wisely.

# CHAPTER 9

As well as the necessary traps, snowshoes and warm winter garb, Carson bought himself a new Sharps rifle, 50 calibre, and a .44 Colts Dragoon as a side arm. In the mountains there was bigger and more dangerous game than on the Plains, and he wanted to be properly armed to deal with whatever the future held for him there. it would not be easy he knew, but even more difficult if he failed to carry with him every little necessity he could think of.

For the next five years Carson came out of the mountains with prime plews[36] and pelts in abundance. Beaver, otter, muskrat, coyote, wolf, wolverine and bear. Mink, pine martin, raccoon, lynx and mountain lion. If it moved and had fur there was a market for it. Even the humble raccoon pelt was worth a dollar, and for Carson, every dollar earned was a dollar saved towards his dream. Every day brought its disappointments too, and the trap lines were long, lonely and dangerous for a man alone.

Many a trapper just simply disappeared, and his disappearance remained a mystery. He could have been murdered for his pelts, and that was always a possibility. He could have been killed and eaten by a bear, and grizzly were particularly dangerous. He could have been injured and unable to make it back to his cabin, or if inexperienced or careless he could have been lost in a whiteout[38] and perished with cold.

There were just so many ways a trapper could become a victim. Carson knew this and always carried flint, steel and tinder for fire, and a piece of smoked fish, pemmican, or meat for overnight sustenance. A light canvas roll, waterproofed with bear grease would turn the worst of a blizzard in an emergency, and completed his preparations. He did not carry much water, as it was too heavy, and snow would provide his needs on that score.

If very badly injured he knew all was lost, and there was nothing he could do to prevent that except be careful. Carson was careful!

It was hard and constant work. No trap line could be trapped two years in succession, at least not by responsible trappers. This meant that each season a new line must be opened, and that meant hard work, axe work, brush clearing work. When a line was ready it was many miles long, and every day traps must be set, and traps already set regularly checked before any carcass fell to predators.

When trapped, each carcass must be skinned out and the hide scraped to remove any flesh before stretching it on the frames or boards to dry. Bitterly cold every day and lonely every night, trapping was not for the fainthearted, but he stuck with it, for it was rewarding, and to his thinking much more likely to provide for his future than prospecting.

In prospecting, there was too much of the element of gambling. That chance scrape that would uncover the riches, or disappoint once again the fevered seeker, and send him on to another search, another disappointment. Trapping was different Carson thought, for here in the mountains there was fur, and fur could always be trapped or shot!

He was already in the mountains two years before he found the letter! While working on a beaver pelt one evening, Carson first became aware of his family history, of a scandal that preceded the migration of his parents to this wild and distant wilderness. As he was hanging the finished beaver pelt on its frame near the cabin wall, his elbow caught and dislodged an old leather satchel that had lain on a shelf since he had moved in. The satchel contained the papers old Zack had given him out of his father's trunk, and Carson had never shown much interest in them by way of close scrutiny.

He had been distracted with the sudden provision of his grubstake, and had neglected the papers and documents in favour of the gold. He felt suddenly ashamed of this, as he saw his father's last possessions scattered on the floor unopened, and as he pondered on it he was led to see just how easily a heart can be deceived, and eyes blinded to decency and responsibility by the colour of riches. He had been in this cabin now two years, and never once thought of reading the last correspondence his dead father had left.

Wiping the blood off his hands, he gathered the papers off the floor and carried them to the table, whereon sat an oil lamp whose light struggled feebly against the darkness and gloom of his trapper dwelling. Leafing through the documents, they were as he thought. An assortment of papers that no doubt were important to his father, but held little value for him.

Old mortgage papers. The sale of their home in Plymouth. A list of patients and their treatments. An old Court summons relevant to some inquest or other back in England, and a recipe for the treatment of the Ague. There were a few more smaller items of no interest to him, and he was about to wrap all up again when an old and stained envelope among them took his attention. With an address from Scotland and a date just before Carson was born, it was a lengthy treatise on a scandal that had overshadowed the family in Rannoch. It was from his grandmother, and the letter was to his father, and left no stone unturned in the account of the scandal. Her husband's brother, Carson's grand uncle, Magus Carson, had been accused of murder. As Carson read the now decades-old letter, he became absorbed in it, and, bad as the light was, he was not deterred from reading every last word.

*"Dear Jason,*

*Got your last letter safe, and glad that Helen is well and looking forward to the childbirth. We are still in Rannoch and doing well as far as our health goes. Your father's sight has worsened somewhat and so I am writing this for him.*

*We wouldn't be troubling you now with this letter but for a very great change in our family life that happened just two months ago. Even though it was never spoken of when you were here, and we tried to keep it from you, you must know something of the accusation made against your father's brother Magus when you were but a child of five years.*

*I will now tell the story from beginning to end, for after all these years it has finally ended well, and you might be able to bring it to an end even better for your father's sake, for it has been a cross for him to bear these many long years.*

*When Magus was a young man of 19 or 20, he was out one night after the salmon. He and a few others were down at Claggan Bridge pool and were running a net across when the Laird and two of his gamekeepers came upon them. In the darkness, a shot was fired and they were called upon to surrender, but instead they scattered and ran, leaving the net and the fish they had already caught. The story we got from the gamekeepers was that one of the poachers lifted a rock and struck the Laird, killing him instantly. It was a terrible night for us all, and the whole village here was in mourning at the tragedy.*

*No one knew for sure who any of the men were, for in the darkness it was impossible to identify them, but the next day at first light when the keepers and some men went back to the scene, they found a small ticket, a cobbler's token with a number on it for a pair of boots left for repair.*

*The Magistrate's men went to Farquhar the cobblers with the token, and the name in the ledger against that number was Magus Carson. From that very moment, your uncle Magus was a dead man. Even before they left the cobbler's shop, they had vowed revenge, and hanging was their ultimate aim.*

*Simon Farquar, the cobbler, a friend of Magus, and not believing for a moment that he had been involved in this killing, immediately sent his boy Ian to find Magus and tell him to run, for they were after him for the Lairds death, and a rope awaited him if caught.*

*Thankfully Magus did run. He took to the hills which he knew so well, and by that means made his way to the Clyde, where he found shipping to the New World.*

*We never heard from him since, but a local man who returned to Rannoch from the frontier after several years, told us a story of a white man whose name was often spoken of around the campfires in the Sierra. A man of 'great strength and stature' so he said, and who was known to live among the Indians of those parts, and even to have married one and had a family. Can that happen out there Jason? Could this be true, or do you think it is only a story?*

*Your father has mourned every day since Magus left, and the news we have just had recently has indeed caused him to lift his head again for his long-lost brother.*

*The second of those gamekeepers has died, the first, William McHenry, having died many years ago. Gregor McNickle was the second to die, and before he died he sent for his minister and the Lairds great-grandson and made a complete and signed confession as to what happened that night at Claggan Bridge pool.*

*He said that he and William McHenry, the other keeper, with the Laird, surprised three men fishing on the pool. The Laird fired his pistol in the air as a means of frightening them into surrender, but they scattered and ran. At no time did the poachers come into contact with the Laird and the keepers. The Laird was killed due to a very simple and common accident. He stumbled in the haste of the moment and struck his head on a rock. He was already dead when they went to assist him.*

*Angry that the poachers had got away, and ashamed that their employer and master was killed in their very presence, the two keepers made up the story of the attack, as it would look better for them in the community. McNickle said that he could not go to his maker with that guilt on his soul, and a notice was put on the church gates and a few public buildings as a token of reparation to your uncle Magus, and as an encouragement to us as a family.*

*Magus might be still alive, in his 80s now, and your*

*father would like you to make some enquires as to this story our neighbour told us, and if found alive tell Magus he is a free man.*

*Take care son. Tell Helen we will be praying for a safe delivery for her.*

*God bless and keep you safe.*

*Your loving mother Eliza."*

Carson sat for a very long time with this letter in his hand. There was nothing else. He even checked the satchel again in hope of finding more of this correspondence, but there was nothing. Once again, he reproached himself for neglecting to properly examine his father's papers. He had lost two years of that neglect, but he determined now to do what he could to solve this mystery, and he would find satisfaction in doing so.

# CHAPTER 10

First cleaning the glass of the lamp, and trimming the wick to burn smoothly, he arranged all that old Zack had given him on the table and laid it there in order. His grandmother's letter to his father was central to it all, and from that he must piece together the story. He had no means of verifying anything he might deduce, but he had to try.

There before him was the last of the gold nuggets in the old piece of cloth, a small handful. The money belt from England, the little signed card with his father's sailing date, and the old papers that had hidden the letter so well.

From the letter he deduced that he had kin on the frontier. Not close kin it was true, but kin just the same. Again, the letter pinpointed just where his kin might be if still alive. The far West, and a very possible connection with the Indians.

He had also the approximate year that Magus had fled. It was when his father was around five years old. That would make him now in his eighties if he was still alive.

As Carson surveyed the bits and pieces on the table, he considered them individually and closely. These items alone could help him. The bag, and the gold it contained. The panned gold, river gold old Zack said, strange gold for the Powder River area.

Pulling the old cloth towards him he shook the nuggets from it and, taking his knife, he scraped what grime and dirt he could from it until the original woollen weave showed more clearly. It was as he had always thought. A dark green, but with a red line, inter-crossed with a yellow or golden thread, and forming a pattern of squares.

The revelation then struck him like a lightning bolt! *It was tartan.* Scottish tartan. His father's gold was wrapped in tartan. Sierra Gold. A grand uncle fleeing to the Sierras. His grandmother's letter naming a possible Indian marriage, and his own father having this gold in his medical bag on returning from visiting Indians!

Carson did not rule out coincidence in any offhand way, but he had a very real belief in facts. In his way of thinking if the facts coincided with coincidence, it became providence! What he had therefore on the table was the means of the mystery being unravelled. There was only one area left to consider Carson thought, and there would be no sleep until it was done.

One issue alone, if solved, would complete the picture he had already constructed in his mind, and it was the night the four Indians came to the cabin door. What brought them was always a mystery to him. Why, he now thought, was the visit made, and the request for the doctor to go with them, only settled by a small piece of paper passed from them to him? What was in the note that finally persuaded the doctor to go with them, and feel safe in doing so?

Carson thought long and hard about this.

There had never been an Indian at the cabin door before, and as far as he could remember, there had never been another since! It was that first visit that changed the doctor's pattern of living. It was from that first visit his regular journeys to the Indians began, and they continued over many years. Looking back now Carson could see they were never a chore to his father. Never a burdensome or tiresome duty. Indeed, it was the very opposite. These visits were a looked forward to event, a source of anticipated enjoyment.

Carson only remembered disjointed snatches of those early journeys. He remembered the uncomfortable buggy rides, where he would fall asleep and awake to ask, "Is it far now?"

His father would laugh at this and tell him that the next time he slept, he would wake up there. As he grew older, he took a greater interest in those journeys, and always remembered that when the trail came to a creek or a river his father would first drive the buggy into the water to let the horse drink, then, if the water was deep enough, he would unhitch the pony to allow the wheels to soak. He would give them a half turn midway through his halt, and this would ensure that each wheel got equally covered. The water he said "made the wheels to be stronger, 'cause when the spokes were tightened by the water, they were not so easily broken or damaged."

Sometimes on a very long journey they would take a picnic, and eat beside a stream or creek. Often while his father got a fire going for coffee, Carson would take a swim or bathe in the cooling, rippling flow.

He never forgot the sight of those Indian encampments as they first came into view. Tepees stretching for miles he thought, and the smoke from their fires rising slowly like soft blue streamers, slanting away downwind only to be lost where the prairie met the sky.

Carson could have remained in this state of reverie, for those memories had become more precious to him as his mind slowly healed after the accident, and every little remembrance from that time he treasured greatly.

However, his grandmothers letter caused him to look back now with a more inquisitive eye, and seek to unravel the mystery it had uncovered. He tried to remember his father treating sick or ailing Indians on those visits, and to his great surprise he found he had not one single recollection of such except for the Great Elk incident when he fell from the tree. Always when they would arrive his father would make an inquiry from whoever was at hand and then make his way to the tepee of Many Horses, Great Elks father.

Many Horses would come to greet him and chase the boys away to play as he did so. Carson was never inside the tepee of Many Horses, for on those visits he played and ate and slept with his young companions, and an old woman looked after them.

The Chief's tepee was always on the outer edge of any camp, and in the afternoons and evenings Carson could see his father and Many Horses with another man sitting round their own campfire. The other man was tall yet stooped, with long silvery hair that came past his shoulders, and mingling with an even more silvery beard that fell upon his chest.

As Carson looked again at the assortment of pieces upon the table and brought to bear his present recollections on them, only now did the significance of the bearded figure strike the young trapper. Those Indians never grew facial hair, yet the old man was heavily bearded.

Carson suddenly stiffened as the revelation took hold. *His father had found his uncle,* and Chief Many Horses was his son. Great Elk, his young playmate, was a grandson. The whole picture now flooded his mind, a mind that almost refused to accept it. The tartan cloth, a piece of an old plaid. The Sierra gold in the doctor's bag the day he was killed! The Indians did not give his father the gold as old Zack had thought, his uncle Magus had given it, and generously too.

As Carson rolled back the years, he now saw things he had never questioned before. Why did his father always take settler food on his journeys?

Food separate from the picnic food. As a child it had not interested him, but now it became a telling clue to the relationship he suspected he had uncovered.

Cheeses, oven bread, a side of salt pork. Fruit when available, and flour too.

That was why the doctor went out that night with four strangers and told his wife it was safe to do so. The young injured man was a relative of Magus, or a son of a friend, and Magus, revealing his whereabouts, and his secret of decades, had sent the note to his nephew as a last desperate means to save his life. Carson supposed that his grandmother's letter had perhaps already planted the thought in his father's mind of his uncle living among the Indians, and so the note needed no verification when it was produced.

It all made so much sense now that it could not possibly mean anything else.

With all this now in his understanding, his thoughts turned to his boyhood friend Great Elk, and the secret pact he made that day by mingling their blood.

Great Elk was not initiating a new bond when he pricked their thumbs, he was confirming an *existing bond*. Great Elk *knew* the secret of his grandfather, and the blood bond that was already between himself and Carson!

# CHAPTER 11

The dawn was breaking through the tops of the pines that encircled his cabin before Carson rose from the table and stirred last night's embers, setting the coffee pot over the growing flame. His nights' work had brought him great satisfaction. He thought he had accomplished personal fulfilment when old Zack had given him his father's papers and effects, but it was nothing like this. This would be something that would be part of his life as long as he had life, and the thought pleased him.

He was sure his father had communicated the finding of Magus to those back home in Scotland, and if his Grand uncle was still alive, and it was just possible, he would be in his nineties now. He had last seen Great Elk around 13 years ago, before the accident that killed his parents had brought their relationship to a sudden end. Thirteen years. Thirteen uncertain and dangerous years for the Indian people. He might even be dead, but if not, where would he begin to look for him in this vast wilderness?

The coffee pot lid was now rattling, and as Carson took his first sip in many hours he did so as one who now felt a new strength of character, a sense of belonging, a very real connection to this great land and its people. Never again would he feel the guilt of being a white intruder. In a very real sense, the Indians were now his people, for he had family among them.

Although Carson became an experienced and successful trapper, he was so for a reason. This was his chosen profession for this period of his life, but it was never his life in itself. He never forgot the day-old Zack introduced him to the possibility of a hunting career. He never forgot the idea and the possibilities, and often mulled it over in his mind.

He had travelled far from that first day with Zack. He was a natural shot, it was evident, and he always experienced a deep, inner satisfaction of finding his beast lying inert and still. Majestic in life, even in death it had a beauty. An object of his respect, and with a gratefulness for the opportunity, he counted it a privilege to take it and use it for his necessary provision. He took pride in his ability to fulfil this role, and in claiming his own possession, won through his field craft and marksmanship. Sport shooting could never compare with what Carson felt in those moments. Sport had no part in Carson's quest for fresh meat. He could not explain it, but he could feel it. No matter how many times his rifle proved true, the first sight of his kill never failed to stir these same emotions. As he began to prepare a carcass he often smiled at the memory of Zack's demonstration, for he had now the mastery of the knife, and he still had all his fingers!

Unlike many up here in the mountains Carson was not a recluse, nor was he an individual that could not survive peaceably among his fellow men. Many trappers were just so. They lived alone and died alone for the sole reason that they found it difficult to co-exist within organised society. Carson always had an end in sight throughout his lonely years, and after the fifth winter it was time to call it a day and move on.

With his inheritance, and his five years trapping, he had enough for his horse ranch now, build a good home, and afford to import a stud animal of some pedigree to begin his herd. Things were moving forward on the frontier and he wanted to move with the times. The Cavalry were always needing good remounts, something better than the mustangs[39] the Indians rode. With the railroad a direct link back East, he could foresee the day when it would become a thriving avenue of commerce, the prairies providing for the hungry mouths of the ever-growing civilisation on the eastern seaboard, and the finer things of life coming west in return. Carson wanted to be prepared when that day would come, and he was ready to settle down.

The Homestead Act of 1862 could not have come at a more opportune time. He had already filed a claim on his allowed 160 acres, and, with his cabin now built, in five years he could claim the Title Deed. He was now almost 30 years old, what he made of the future was down to him.

With the paperwork done he took on work that would ensure his being reasonably near what would be his future home, and just as Zack had said, he found it readily. Men like Carson who knew the country were always in great demand, either as army scouts, guides or hunters, and often it was just such men who prevented the settlers from losing their scalps!

 It was during this period that Carson found himself a wife, a beautiful Arapaho girl called Prairie Flower. Scouting one day for hostiles, he came across a large band of Arapahos on the move, following the buffalo. As was his habit, if he encountered 'friendlies' he always made it his business to talk with them, for he found that much of the local trouble between settlers and Indians was lack of communication and a too itchy trigger finger!

Carson was known among them, they knew who he was, and they respected him. It felt it natural to him therefore to spend some time in their various camps and partake of their hospitality. He was after all used to tepee living. It was on one such occasion that Prairie Flower caught his eye. Active, lithe and supple, as she gave him his supper her eye lingered a little too long on the Wasi'cu with the long hair and fringed buckskin, and Carson noted it.

After supper, as the elders sat around the fire, Carson made a casual enquiry as to the girl, and came to know she was the daughter of

Running Bear, the Chief now sitting across the fire from him. Before he left next morning he approached Running Bear and told him he would like to give a token of gratefulness in return for the kindness he had been shown, and offered to shoot a few buffalo from the nearby herd as he passed on his way back to the Fort. So began a closer friendship between them, and in the process of time Prairie Flower became his wife.

It was the year 1866, and it was to Prairie Flower, already nursing her own newborn, that Carson now approached with the tiny infant cradled in his cupped hands.

As his ranch house came into view Carson had assured himself that the child was still alive, and to his great satisfaction felt movement beneath his shirt, where the infant had indeed gained some heat during the last few hours on the trail.

Wide-eyed and wondering, Prairie Flower watched her husband cross the puncheon[40] floor with the papoose in his hands, the heavy timbers absorbing silently his every step. "I have a present for you," he said with a smile, as he reached her the little bundle. "She was born about four or five hours ago, so she's gotta be hungry, it's a miracle she's alive at all."

Prairie Flower never questioned her husband's sudden intrusion into the cabin and the unusual gift he delivered, explanations would come later. Frontier life did not lend itself to trivia when action was needed, and so she simply placed her own sleeping infant in the cradle beside her, and, taking the papoose, wrapped her warmly in a shawl, and put her to her breast.

She would wash and clothe her later. Thus, Carson's family doubled within a few hours. Carson called his own girl Helen, after his mother, and he named the foundling Ta-pun-Sa-Win, Lakota[33] for 'Red Cheeked Woman.' She would get Tappy, and when she was old enough to ask how she got her name, he would tell her the story!

# CHAPTER 12

Carson sat on his pony and surveyed the scene before him. Below, a team of buffalo skinners slowly made their way up the valley. The sharp chink of their hammer as it struck the steel spike had a corresponding double when the echo was counted, and the distance made the sound to be out of rhythm with the rise and fall of the action. Carson had watched this all before. It had become a common sight, for it was a lucrative if somewhat dirty business. They called it Hide Hunting.

At around $3.00 for a large hide, when a Union Army private earned only $13 a month, Carson was not surprised at the attraction it held for so many. Some skinners just slashed the hide off the beast, slash by slash, cutting close to the flesh and taking care not to damage the hide itself. Others followed the method he watched below.

Beginning behind the ears, and after making all the necessary skinning cuts, they put a team of horses to it and dragged the hide off, the buffalo's head having been previously spiked and anchored to the ground.

The hunters were nowhere to be seen, having moved on with the herd, leaving a trail of dark mounds here and there on the prairie behind them. The only visible difference between the hunter's work and the skinner's work was the colour of the carcass. When the skinners had finished the carcase glistened white in the sunlight. The layer of fat, built up over the summer, and crucial to the animal's survival in winter, was white, as opposed to beef tallow which was more onto yellow. Buffalo tallow was also very tasty, and sometimes the skinners made a broth with it and drank it against the cold of the Plains in winter.

Yes, Carson saw it all and understood it all, but he didn't like it! Shifting slightly in the saddle, he let his eye take in another scene before him. On a hill to his north, a band of Indians were doing the same thing as Carson, and they didn't like it either! Every white mound the skinners left behind was almost a ton of meat, left to rot upon the prairie, or scavenged by buzzards, coyotes, and wolves. To the Indian this was incomprehensible, and more to the point, unforgivable. To so destroy their sole source of survival and way of life while they looked on only meant one thing. The white man had come to destroy them, and this could only mean war!

Keeping well out of range, for the skinners carried long-range weapons, the Indians surveyed the valley below with heavy hearts, for every pile of drying hides represented a winter's meat for the camp, and warm robes for the wives and children.

Although a frontiersman, Carson had held strong moral values, and a conscience to go with them. His father had been associated with a religious movement in Plymouth England. They were a very plain people, and simply called themselves 'Brethren.' While on the frontier the family did not have opportunity to meet in a public fashion on the Lord's Day, yet his mother had taught the boy herself, and she used the Bible for his reading lessons. The stories Carson had read therefore as a child, and his further religious education by Grandma Turner, had resulted in his character being formed through them, and his life's values built on them.

In the first twenty or so years of his life therefore, Carson had obtained a firm grasp of the origins of the human race, and the husbandry and responsibility of earth's provision as given to them. The thoughts of his heart and his beliefs were in harmony. There was no conflict in his heart on this. There were two sides to life's coin, and Carson was happy within himself at what God had provided on the one hand, and what he had inherited on the other.

This wanton waste and destruction Carson saw below him therefore, and which was taking place in a thousand other places at the same time, Carson knew to be morally wrong, wickedly wrong. So also was the destruction of the Indians themselves. Far greater indeed, for human life, above all life, was sacred.

His mind wandered back to his finding of little Tappy, and his heart warmed at the memory. With the little girl growing up, and with own child Helen, he and Prairie Flower were content, but nevertheless, dark clouds overshadowed them. The story was not hard to unravel.

Gold had been found in Montana, and the nation had been impoverished by the civil war. Hunters, prospectors and settlers in their thousands had been encouraged to come and lay claim to fame and fortune. The most direct and best-watered route to the goldfields and Oregon trail from Fort Laramie was northwest from Nebraska through Wyoming. Most of the trail crossed through land that had been already ceded to the Crow Indian nation in the 1851 treaty, and the Crow themselves had no objection, but this ceded land had now been lost to the Crows by hostile incursions of Sioux, Lakota and Cheyenne, and the victors watched as these Wasi'cu trundled through this their new territory, slaughtering game and leaving the carcasses to rot. It was a sight to stir a heart to resentment, and Carson felt that resentment too.

It was mostly because of his deeply held religious beliefs towards the Indian question that Carson always rode alone in his duties for the Army.

He was not a big man, and he cut an unassuming figure as he sat astride his mount. Well-worn soft buckskins were his preferred mode of dress, and he wore Indian moccasins that came over his calf, laced around with buckskin thongs. He had in his saddle scabbard a big bore Sharps carbine, and, unlike so many more riflemen, he refrained from changing, or being distracted by other models and makes that seemed to be constantly appearing. He had learned to stick with what worked well for him, and nothing worked better than the Sharps.

Unlike lighter calibres, it's .50 calibre slug was heavy enough to allow for reasonable adverse windage without the inconvenience and nuisance of constant correction, and if the barrel could be rested for the shot, even at long range, it could repeat the same performance again and again with unfailing regularity. The Sharps was noted for its accuracy, and yet its accuracy lay in this simplicity, the calibre, and the consistent steady hand of the shooter.

Carson knew the secret of good hunting lay in two facts. The shooter must first of all know what his rifle could do, and, knowing that, know then what he could do with his rifle! Overconfidence in either of these was sure to fail.

As a sidearm he carried a Colts Dragoon, .44 Calibre, and the powder loads he used were capable of knocking a man over at 80 yards, more than sufficient in any hostile scenario he could envisage himself in. A bowie knife and a well-packed saddle roll completed his arsenal, for Carson was a scout, not an infantry soldier, and the weapons were carried mainly to hunt, rather than for a prolonged engagement under fire.

With his ammunition safely wrapped in his saddlebags, Carson always carried a few spare loads wrapped securely in his pocket should he get separated from his horse in a hostile situation, but his wits and wisdom always guided him to avoid hostile situations! Although armed for protection, Carson held no animosity towards the Indians, and this was one of the reasons why he scouted alone.

As far as hunting meat for the army was concerned, with the sole exception of one ex-trooper who had similar skills, held like values, and whom he trusted, he always hunted alone. This decision was an eminently personal and practical one.

Carson took no pleasure in killing. He killed of necessity, therefore when Carson hunted, meat was the objective, and if that meant an animal being killed then that kill shot must be the cleanest and swiftest death he could deliver, and not every hunter had the same philosophy!

To hunt successfully required more than a rifle, a horse, and an open range. When Carson hunted his senses were at their peak. His eyes, his ears, his nose, were all in play, for he knew very well that the wild game he was hunting were likewise doing the same thing! Silence was his best friend when on a hunt, and so alone he could hunt better.

The successful hunter also knew the ways of the hunted, for he took pains to observe them. He knew from long experience that animals were creatures of habit, and as such were predictable, and it was this very predictableness that he often depended on for success. Too many men were careless and indifferent to the realities of finding and killing game cleanly. Impatient, reckless even, they then became a liability. So until the trooper of like mind as himself came along, hunting alone was his first choice, always peaceful, calm, unhurried. Nor was he an advocate of long-range shooting, and he frowned on those that were. A buffalo was a big enough target to hit even at 300 yards, but hitting and killing cleanly were two different things.

Carson took pride in his role as hunter, and a quiet satisfaction in bringing down an animal immediately with a well-placed shot. This was always important to him, not only because Zack taught him, but also because a gut-shot animal would run off and die a lingering death, and where other men would take a chance with a long shot, he preferred to forego a shot rather than lose a beast to perish slowly in great suffering.

In good light and with a barrel rest, 200-250 yards was his very limit, but much closer if he could manage it. Zack's high shoulder shot, the spine-lung area, with the .50 calibre slug, would deliver a humane and powerful strike to enable it to be successful every time.

He took an unspoken pride in seeing his target drop to the shot, and he had good reason to remember how important a clean drop shot was, for he still winced at the memory of being off aim ever so slightly.

He was hunting one morning at first light when he spotted a Whitetail. It was not a long shot but at an awkward angle.

Using his cover tree as a rest for his rifle, he killed it cleanly, but just at that moment another suddenly came into view! It was on high alert and making for cover, and at just over a hundred yards was well within range, even at first light. Carson waited patiently, and as it stopped for that last, predictable, inquisitive look back, he got his chance. Another shot from the same position hit it hard, and it ran into a marshy thicket of second-growth timber.

As Carson examined the spot where the deer disappeared, he saw the bright pink lung blood and tissue on the leafy growth where the ball exited, and knew then that the animal would be dead when he found it. As a matter of fact, he knew from experience it was dead already! Although game was plentiful in the area, he could not simply leave this kill. It took nearly two hours of following the blood trail, cutting his way through brush and second growth saplings, and using deadfalls and rotten branches to cross marshy gully's, before he found it. It took nearly another two hours to extract it back to the trail, as he had to quarter it and carry it out in gunny sacks!

When he was dressing the animal he ran a twig through from the point of impact to where the shot exited. The ball had passed just half an inch below the spine! Half an inch! Yes, Carson had learned his trade by hard-won experience, and he was not about to sacrifice that for the sake of any social benefit a companion might bring. With thoughtless hunting companions, things could become complicated for a wide variety of reasons, and so, always shy of irksome situations or needless controversy, Carson hunted alone.

The reason he rode and scouted alone was more personal, and had its roots in Grandma Turner's diligence and devotion to the young son she said the Lord had brought to her childless cabin.

Scouting alone meant that Carson could interpret for himself whatever situation he might chance upon in his duties. He did not scruple a fair and equal battle between men equipped and ready for it, but he would not be a party to a programme of annihilation of what he considered to be an already wronged people, his people, and most certainly not the wanton slaughter of women and children. He could never put his hand to that, for he knew *"The Lord had made of one blood all nations"*. Every man therefore had the right to enjoy what God had so generously provided for them. To him, might was not necessarily right, and so he rode alone. He would be the master of his own destiny, and not another.

## CHAPTER 13

Although Carson was well on his way to being settled, with a wife and two children to provide for, 1866 had brought no betterment to the growing problem of the Indians. The Indians and the problems they presented were always included in every conversation at some stage or other, even if the conversation was about the latest fashion from Paris having been seen on the Sutler's[41] wife's head at church last Sunday!

The Indian issue had always been there since the white man came, for very early on it became a pretty well-established belief in political circles that until the Indian was removed or rendered ineffective as a fighting force, the whites would never have the land for peaceful settlement. There would be no sharing, and the greed of one would eventually overcome the need of the other.

A comparatively recent event however had brought the situation to a lit fuse on a powder keg, and Carson remembered the event clearly, for he was scouting for the army at the time.

The Indians had harried and pressed the invader of their lands at every opportunity. When Mormon settlers moved into northern Utah, the traditional hunting ground for the Shoshone, their sheer numbers caused the superintendent of Indian Affairs, Jacob Forney, to write to the Department of the Interior in 1859 stating,

*"The Indians… have become impoverished by the introduction of a white population."*

He recommended that a reserve be established for the preservation of the already depleted essential resources for the Shoshone. This was ignored by his superiors. When the game was gone there was only starvation remaining. In 1862, James Doty, the then Superintendent of Indians Affairs spent four days assessing the situation and wrote,

*"The Indians have been in great numbers, in a starving and destitute condition. No provisions having been made for them, either as to clothing or provisions by my predecessors."*

All this was common knowledge at the Sutlers. Mackintosh, who owned the store, heard everything, saw everything, and got newspapers regularly from back East. Carson, as hunter, scout, and interpreter was himself well placed to hear at first - hand what the situation was. The Civil war and the governmental upheaval concerning it were blamed by many to be the reason for this neglect of the Indian's dilemma, but it was in reality a lame excuse. The real reason was much nearer to home!

All too often the Indian harassment had ended in bloodshed. Settlers, both men, women and children lost their lives in these attacks, and the mutilations were something that even the frontier-hardened Carson found hard to accept, or even to understand. But when those same atrocities, like the one he came across when he found the little infant, became normal for both sides, he was appalled. The savage may be excused for his behaviour, but when civilised men take on the mantle of the savage, wherein lies civilisation?

The situation could not continue as it was, and it could only have one end! The ignoring of previous treaties with the Indians, sometimes the ink had hardly dried on the documents, and the trespassing and plundering of their ceded lands of its buffalo herds and mineral deposits, all became too much for the goodwill of the tribes to endure.

When eventually the Indians fought back, a series of Forts were built along the Bozeman trail to protect the white trespasser, and to bring the Indians into submission to each new Government betrayal!

Although Carson worked for the army, he could never countenance such an obvious programme of ongoing humiliation, deceit and bloodshed. He would save army life where and when he could, that he had sworn to do, but he would remain his own man when it came to his conscience.

Sometimes warning of danger, and sometimes detouring a company of Cavalry around it. But he could never report on a group of women and children, or view them as a threat, and lead the Cavalry to massacre them. The Bear River incident of 1863 was just an example of what Carson viewed as this government-sponsored destruction.

Further west on the Oregon trail, towards Fort Hall and the Wind River country, things were not good, and Carson knew that the situation would one day lead to tragedy. That the innocent would pay for the guilty would be a certainty, for innocence or guilt did not figure when the US Army set out to punish Indians.

After some years of food raids, with wagon trains and miners attacked, many lives lost and property stolen, the Shoshone people at last brought the might of Government forces against them.

It mattered not that these Indian raids were for survival rather than revenge, or that being *"destitute and in starvation,"* was an excuse. Nor indeed that Superintendent Doty had personally spent four days among them and gave a first-hand account of their pitiful condition.

It was Colonel Patrick Edward Conner who led the punitive raid on a winter encampment, and the fact these men were peaceful bands of Indians did not appear to have been considered.

On January 29, 1863, heavy snow and bitterly cold conditions assailed the hard-pressed and hungry Shoshone. Encamped in a willow brake, they were eking out an existence on the minimum of provision, and seeking to find what shelter they could from winter's icy blast. Their children were the most grievously affected. Poorly clad and ill-fed, their plight was a constant source of grief, and many died that winter. It was upon this ill-fated band that government forces, totalling around 300, all well-armed, and with two howitzers in tow with abundant ammunition, were sent on their errand of destruction.

Coming upon the Shoshone encampment, at the confluence of the Bear River and Battle Creek, they attacked. Initially the Indians fought bravely and successfully, for they had scouts out too and so had been warned of danger, but they ran out of ammunition after about two hours, whereupon the better armed and mobilised soldiers inflicted a total and merciless defeat, killing around 300 men, women and children and capturing around 160 more.

It was carnage, and a carnage that was to be enacted exactly ten months later, November 29, 1864, when a company of Colorado Volunteers, led by Colonel John Chivington[42], fell upon an unsuspecting encampment of Indians, and slaughtered men, women and children indiscriminately. Hundreds died. The Indians, Cheyenne and Arapaho, were camped in the vicinity of US Fort Lyon, waiting on Treaty arrangements to be finalised, and thought they were safe. Even though a special panel was set up to investigate this action, and found Chivington and his men guilty of cold-blooded murder, no one was ever punished for it.

It was atrocities like these, cruel and unjust in the extreme, and directed at women and children in particular, that led to even greater reprisals by the Indians, and one in particular stands out in history, when the Indians inflicted the greatest ever casualties on US Army troopers up to that time.

It became known as the Fetterman Massacre. Carson knew Fetterman, indeed he knew all those that fell that day, and although greatly saddened at the loss of life, he was not at all surprised. The young cavalry officer in conversation had asked Carson one day did he hate the Indian. Whereupon Carson replied, "I don't hate the Indian Mr Fetterman. Right now I can get by with being plenty scared of them, for the first one to make a mistake gets to diggin' graves".

Carson meant it, he meant every word of it, and Fetterman had brought those words to pass with the loss of his entire company.

# CHAPTER 14

As Carson considered again the immediate evens that led to the massacre of Fetterman and his company, and he considered it often, he had also reconsidered his responsibility as his scout and advisor. But there was nothing more he could have done. If Fetterman was willing to overrule his commanding officer, how could a lowly scout, clad in buckskins and smelling of buffalo, hope to turn him from the path of destruction?

Yet he promised well at the beginning. A handsome young officer from a military family, clean cut and sporting a handlebar moustache with sideburns, he came to Fort Phil Kearney with impeccable recommendations.

Having been turned down from West Point at eighteen years old, he began his military career eight years later on May 14, 1861, as a first lieutenant in the newly formed 18th US Infantry, a regiment established just ten days earlier by Abe Lincoln himself, and later ratified by Congress. He rose through the ranks rapidly and was in the thick of the action throughout the Civil War.

On the last day of 1862 the 18th Infantry engaged Confederate forces at Stones River Tennessee, and in a four-day battle almost thirteen thousand Union soldiers, and twelve thousand Confederates, lost their lives. Fetterman's 18th lost 300 men, or half its strength in an hour of conflict. For his part, Fetterman received a brevet of Major for gallantry and good conduct during the engagement.

Fetterman's last Civil War action was the Battle of Jonesboro, on September 1, 1864, when Atlanta fell to Union forces. Again, the regiment suffered heavy losses. At the beginning of the campaign, the regiment numbered 653 officers and men, but at the end only 210 answered the call. Fetterman again received a brevet of Lieutenant Colonel for great gallantry and good conduct in his action at Atlanta.

All this of course preceded him to Fort Phil Kearny, and his arrival was waited on eagerly and with anticipation, for there is nothing so discouraging to the ranks of fighting men than inaction. The Forts Commanding Officer, Colonel Henry B. Carrington, also looked forward to having Fetterman join them, if for no other reason than he was in great need of officers.

Although not a veteran in the sense of battle experience, (he was an engineer,) Carrington was wise enough to listen to those who had pioneered trails he had yet to travel. However, his cautious approach to the Indian problem was not appreciated by all in the ranks, and the prospect of a Fetterman coming was all the more welcomed by those who were itching for a fight. Receiving a Brevet twice for bravery, unscathed throughout the very worst of the Civil War, Fetterman was a man to follow and listen to!

Fetterman rode into Fort Phil Kearney on November 3, 1866. Within a few days the young officer had his first experience with the Indians, and within forty-eight hours, November 5, had approached Carrington with a plan to outwit the Sioux!

Fetterman's plan was so at variance with what Carrington knew of the Indians' cunning that he agreed to let him implement it. Perhaps he thought a lesson taught by experience would be better than advice.

The plan involved hobbling some mules in plain sight as live bait. When the Indians approached to steal them the hidden Cavalry detachment would break cover and deal with them! After a long and sleepless night shivering in the trees, the detachment returned to the Fort, tired and weary, only to hear the news that the Indians had stolen a settler's cattle just a mile distant! Fetterman was enraged. He had been outwitted in his very first military strategy!

Just two days later, on November 7, his second introduction to the Indians took place. While familiarising himself with the locality in the presence of a few officers, they visited the nearby woods where an army wood-cutting operation was underway.

Fetterman and the other officers, riding too far ahead of their escort, came under fire in a ravine by around 15–20 Indians armed with rifles. Despite two volleys being fired at them from about 50 paces, they remained unscathed and were able to return fire and regroup with their escort.

This incident was a most unfortunate event, for the young officer, instead of giving due consideration to the antiquity of those rifles fired by the Indians, and their lack of opportunity and powder supply to become proficient with them, became even more depreciative of the Indians' competence in arms. His own prejudiced opinion of the Indians' poor fighting ability was therefore strengthened. His increasing disrespect became well known in the Fort, and he was now more impatient than ever to "settle accounts."

Carson heard his boasts. *"A company of regulars could whip a thousand, and a regiment could whip the whole array of hostile tribes."*

Carson could have told him that the Great Plains were already dotted with the graves of those who thought the same, but he held his peace. The young Civil War hero must learn for himself, for he would not be told!

Refused a request by Carrington to chastise Red Cloud and the Sioux with fifty regulars and fifty civilians, and at odds with his commanding officer for his perceived leniency to the Sioux raids, Fetterman wrote to a friend on November 26, that *"the regiment was afflicted with an incompetent commanding officer."*

He had not yet been at the Fort a month!

It was December 21, and with Christmas at hand, Carson was hunting buffalo for the Fort's larder when he heard the news.

He remembered the day in detail, for he had rerun it a thousand times in his mind, such was the shock the news brought. He had two animals loaded already and was directing the wagon to the location of a third when they noted a rider coming at full gallop towards them. They were five miles from the Fort and they knew something must be greatly amiss when a galloper had been sent to them. It was the Sutler's eldest son, a fine young man, and all too willing to be of any service to the troopers when opportunity arose. His horse lay back on its haunches as he slid to a halt beside them, and in a breathless outburst managed to convey his message in a very few words, "Fetterman's dead. His whole company wiped out."

The hair had stood on Carson's neck as he took in this message. He had seen those men that very morning as they readied themselves to take to the field. They were laughing, grumbling, joking, and some of them were even singing at the prospect of a little exercise and excitement. Now they were all dead according to the galloper. It hardly seemed possible, even to Carson, who knew all too well that the frontier was full of such surprises and tragedies every day. The news the galloper brought had halted the hunting that day, and it was with heavy hearts that they prepared to return. Collecting first the third beast Carson had killed, they made for the Fort, eager to hear more of the tragedy and how it could have happened.

When the meat detail eventually got back in late afternoon, they were just in time to see the relief column that had been sent to Fetterman, bring in 49 bodies. By the time they had arrived at the site of the battle, it was all over and the Indians were long gone. Carson himself scouted for Colonel Carrington next day as he led out a recovery party to bring in the remainder. Stripped naked, mutilated, weapons and horses now in the hands of the Indians, it was a sobering sight indeed.

On Christmas Eve, when even an Army garrison can celebrate and enjoy a little relaxation, the scenes inside Fort Phil Kearney had been far from jubilant. Carson had watched in disbelief as the bodies of Fetterman and Captain Fredrick Brown, another hothead, were buried in the same grave without so much as a bugle note, religious service, or military honours. If Carrington meant to show his disgust at the needless loss of the company, the burials said it all.

After the burials, Carson had made his way to the Sutler's store. He was going home for Christmas, for he missed his girls and Prairie Flower, but he wanted the story before he went, and he knew exactly where to get it. Mackintosh did not disappoint him, but his account made Fetterman's actions that day unforgivable.

A wood detail had been attacked early that morning not far from the Post, and Carrington had ordered a relief party led by Captain Powell.

Fetterman had objected to Powell's appointment on the grounds that he himself had seniority, and Carrington assented. Under strict instructions to relieve the wood detail, and not to engage the Indians, it was impressed upon Fetterman that under no circumstances was he to pursue the hostiles at the expense of the wood train, and certainly not to pursue them over Lodge Trail Ridge, where they would be out of sight of the Fort and the nearby protection it offered.

Before the column left the Fort, apparently Carrington had halted the column, and from a sentry platform at the Fort gate he repeated his instructions about Lodge Trail Ridge.

However, the Colonel's instructions had fallen on deaf ears. Disregarding the older and wiser man's counsel, not to mention his military seniority, Fetterman was seen to take a different trail than that which led to the woodcutters, and in pursuance of his own plan, allowed himself to be goaded by around ten young Indian braves who showed themselves just out of range, taunting the column. In his ignorance of Indian warfare, Fetterman was blinded to what surely must have been an obvious, amateurish decoying tactic, and a thinking man would have seen it at once.

But when it came to Indians Fetterman had not been a thinking man. It would be the last mistake he would ever make. In crossing Lodge Trail Ridge to chase ten, he was ambushed by perhaps 1,500–2,000 hostiles and never stood a chance. It was over in minutes.

The interesting thing was that only 6 bodies out of the 81 slain showed signs of gunshot wounds, and two of them were suspected as self-inflicted! Carson often pondered this fact. Even with the Cavalry having been issued with the new Spencer[43] repeating rifle, the onslaught of numbers overran them in minutes, and the new rifle in such circumstances could never have saved them. Clubbing and arrow wounds seemed to be the main cause of death, preceding the mutilations. It was through such ignorance of Indian combat that prompted Jim Bridger,[44] himself at the Fort at that time, to voice his opinion, *"Them boys know nothing of Indian fighting."*

When the bodies were recovered Fetterman's head was almost severed, while Captain Fredrick Brown's right temple showed powder burns round a bullet hole. Rather than be taken alive he had saved a bullet for himself. He had often stated he would do so, and it did not come as a surprise therefore when the news became known.

That Fetterman was brave is without question, but Carson often wondered where the line should be drawn between bravery and crass stupidity!

The massacre of Fetterman's company was the single greatest loss of life through conflict with the Indians at that time. Carson was not to know that in a few years, the same arrogance and disobedience would lead to a similar massacre, only on a much greater scale!

# CHAPTER 15

Carson had told no one of finding the papoose. Not even his own hired hand. He was careful in his dealings with his fellow men, including the troopers. Jealously and suspicion was rife on the frontier, especially concerning any association with the Indians. When he found the infant, he rode straight to his home. People assumed that Prairie Flower had twins, so close were the births, and Carson let the assumption become the actual story. He did not wish to deceive, nor indeed did he mean to deceive, but so strong was the assumption that after the Fetterman disaster, they felt it wiser in the circumstances to hold their counsel on the facts, and allow the child's origins to remain a family secret.

He had asked to see the report sheet of any recent patrols in his absence when he returned to Fort Phil Kearney, and the written record was far from what the evidence on the ground had told him.

Fetterman had made a brief report concerning a small band of hostiles his detail had surprised in camp. In the encounter that followed they had only lost one horse and two troopers wounded. None of the hostiles survived.

The report was never questioned, for it had become the practice in any engagement to destroy completely the Indian threat, and to do that women and infants must be included!

Few however liked to state so in written form, preferring to use wording that was ambiguous and misleading. The word 'hostiles' was therefore widely used, and served very well to cover the most shameful atrocities.

It had been a somewhat subdued Christmas for Carson. He tried hard not to allow personal likes or dislikes to colour necessary relationships, and spoil that mutual frontier unity so vital to life itself sometimes. But the loss of 81 men lay heavy on his heart. He had even contemplated quitting the army work, and throwing himself into the horse ranch he had taken such great pains to build.

Those few days at home were days therefore of intense reflection, as he considered his circumstances, his home life, and his future.

With his father's gold the old couple had given him, and the cash from his parent's estate, plus the five years trapping he had done, he had been enabled to set himself up with a home of his own, and the small spread would keep him and his in reasonable comfort.

He was not a man attracted to the finery or architecture of the East. The ease of lavish living that motivated so many had too often proved a snare, and in pursuit of which hundreds, nay thousands had perished on the trail from Fort Laramie on the way to the goldfields in Montana. Carson's home was built for survival.

The construction was of sturdy pine logs, barked, smoothed, and notched carefully at each corner, its ridgepole extending well beyond the walls to carry a roof that allowed for a generous overhang, and its four foundation logs rested on crushed rock and small stones taken from the river nearby. Kept off the dampness of the earth they would outlast Carson. A puncheon[45] floor was put in before they began the walls, and it too would never need replacing.

The roof was well covered with shingle, it was not cedar, which could not be had at that time, but it would do, and could always be replaced in a few years when needed.

A large root cellar underneath completed the cabin, and a clapboard[47] barn provided shelter for his wagon, winter feed, tools and supplies. Since he could not spend time on the actual building, Carson had left it in the hands of an old trapper he knew. The trapper was biding his time around the Fort waiting to go back to the mountains in the fall. Carson had done a deal with him. Supervise the men building my cabin and my traps and mountain gear are yours! It was a good deal for both men. Traps were expensive, and Carson had no more use for his!

Prairie Flower had brought an old Indian squaw with her to the cabin, so she was not lonely, and Carson had the added comfort of knowing that in his many and long absences, his hired hand would always be there to assist in any great difficulty that arose.

The hired hand was the result of another deal, and it gave him great satisfaction to contemplate it all again.

Like so many circumstances in life, it happened quite by chance. One day, as Carson was having a shoe re-seated on his horse, a stranger approached the forge. Ignoring the blacksmith he spoke directly to Carson.

"I have been told you own a ranch near here mister, and I have a wagon, team and some fittin's to sell. Would you be interested?"

Carson looked at the man and the boy standing by his side. The man was not above forty and the lad could not have been more than twelve or thirteen. He had seen him pull the wagon out of the line a few days ago as the last train was passing, and wondered what had happened.

"California is yet a long way off stranger, you are going to need your wagon and fittin's when you get there," Carson replied.

The man kicked at the dust with the toe of his boot, and without looking up said slowly,

"California is no longer my destination mister. It was my wife who wanted to go in the first place. We had been settled in Tennessee but she wanted to go west. She had a dream of planting peaches and have the ocean as a backdrop to her orchard. I just wanted her to have the happiness that prospect gave her. But we buried her back at Fort Reno. We lost her to the cholera.

We have no more reason to go on, and nothing to go back to, and I have my boy here to consider. If I could sell my rig, we could rent a place and I could get work. But right now, all I own is in that wagon, and I am strapped for cash."

Carson had looked at the boy and remembered his own misfortune when he was about the same age. But for the old couple's kindness his future could have been much different. There was a moment or two of silence as Carson weighed up the situation, and finally he spoke.

"Wait for me at the store, I'll be along shortly when I have done here." As he had watched the pair walk away, he noted the dejection in their step. All they had dreamed of was gone, and they faced an uncertain future, but if he could help he would do so. Frontier life was hard, but not so hard as the heart that cannot feel for the misfortunes of others!

The blacksmith hammered in the last nail, checked the remaining shoes, and Carson paid him and took his leave. The stranger's wagon was sound and sturdy. Carson was pleased he had chosen the smaller and lighter of the two most common wagons. The larger Conestoga was over 28 feet long and could weigh as much as six tons when loaded. Its rear wheels alone stood at five feet tall, and that left a long stretch of spoke to take the strain of constant swaying and jarring on rough ground. Moreover, it required a team of six animals to pull it, and the trail west took around six months to travel!

In Carson's opinion the Conestoga was just not suitable for such travel, for with the terrain it was just too big, too heavy and too cumbersome.

The stranger had the Prairie Schooner. At only half the size, 12-13 feet, it weighed 1,300 pounds empty, and when loaded about two tons. Lighter and more versatile, it was faster too and could make up to a third more travelling time per day. In good travelling conditions, 20 miles a day.

Well-kept and maintained, it had weathered well since it left Missouri. [48] The mules too were in good shape, with no harness callouses, broken knees, or signs of mistreatment. Here was a man who knew how fragile life on the trail was, and how important it was to take care of those things that life depended on.

Carson had taken a long look inside, for what a man carried said a lot about him. On his travels he had seen pianos, blacksmiths anvils, large and heavy furniture and iron stoves discarded and abandoned along the various trails west. When the animals got weary with the constant, daily workload, and good grazing became in short supply, it was found necessary to off - load every non – essential item if the animals were to continue in harness. This man had packed well and wisely, and he still had his load intact. That's what Carson was looking for.

He noted the usual foodstuffs. Flour, cornmeal, salt, and what was left of a side of bacon packed in a small barrel of bran to keep the heat from spoiling it. Together with other items like lard, tea, coffee, sugar, dried beans and some sliced dried apples and apricots, the man's choices had been good ones. A few cast-iron pots and pans completed the kitchen necessities. He also noted a coil of heavy rope and some chain, with an axe, saw, hammers, axle grease, some spare wagon parts and even a pulley. An iron plough lay on the wagon floor. He didn't see many of those this far on the trail, for they had already been abandoned! There was a lot more besides, but Carson had seen enough. This man had all he needed if he found a place to settle.

Turning to the stranger he spoke kindly to him.

"If you sell this rig you will be left with nothing. For when the money is gone you will have no means to start over, then what will you do?

I tell you what, I'll go good for you in the store over the winter, and if you bring your wagon to my place, you can have a spot where you can build a soddy[49] for you and the boy.

It's down by the river and within sight of my cabin, and a stand of timber close by will provide for building and firewood. The river is full of fish and you can shoot whatever game you choose for the table. Come next spring we will all see the future somewhat better. Don't sell your wagon mister, this may not be California, but it's a grand place to settle."

The man and the boy just stood looking at him, Carson could see it even now as he looked back, and he smiled at the memory. Finally the man said, "How can I repay all this, It's beyond me to think of it mister".

Carson's reply struck him forcibly, "If you can just do as I ask you will not be in my debt, and you can be free to choose if and when you wish to move on. "Ask it then", the man said earnestly, "for I am in your debt already."

"It's not hard to figure," said Carson. "I have a small ranch, and I run and breed a few horses for my cash needs, along with what I can earn as scout and trail guide down here on the Plains. I need someone to see to the ongoing needs of my place. Keeping an eye on the horses, chopping firewood, general maintenance, ploughing and fencing for my wife's garden, that sort of thing.

But more than that. Your soddy will be within sight of my cabin. Half a mile distant for privacy. I want you and your boy to keep an eye out for any strangers, any riders, or for trouble. The Indians do not trouble us, but there are white trash, carpetbaggers, scavengers and outlaws, who are coming west for greed and gain, and they are not particular where they find their wealth. Can you shoot stranger?

"I was at Chickamauga,[50] and at Jonesboro with Fetterman and the 18th, and brought my Spencer with me when I was discharged".

Carson looked hard at the man before him. The mention of Fetterman caused him to ponder, but he held his opinion, and simply replied,

"Well then, you are no stranger to the realities of life and death, so you know what would be expected of you in a hostile situation"

"I know, and I am willing too, just show me where to build my soddy and I will not let you down."

Carson did not regret that transaction, and as he looked back on it again, he thought himself fortunate to have a foreman who could be trusted with all he owned and loved. It was this very knowledge that prompted him to make a decision he would live to be thankful for in later years.

While he loved having a home to return to, he also loved the open trail. The pull of the campfire was strong in him, for every day there was always something new to add interest to living.

He was only thirty-five years old, and so far had been very successful in his horse breeding. He had a contract with the army to supply remounts every year, and now and again someone from back East would come and pick an animal that took their fancy, either for riding or breeding, and who were willing to pay top dollar too. Carson never disappointed his customers, and it was a reputation he was careful to maintain, for on the frontier a man's word was his bond, and trustworthiness was very often the difference between life and death.

Quite apart from his smallholding, Carson was well established in an occupation that few men could do well. Dependable scouts and trail guides were much sought after, and it was not what a man could say of himself that brought in the work, it was what others said of him! This being so he was often named very favourably as wagon master, scout, or advisor in matters relating to the Indians. Carson in other words had a reputation, and although a modest man, and not at all forward, he took something of an inner pleasure in having it!

It was his reputation that had guided Jacob Anderson and his boy Abe to him when they wanted to sell their wagon, and Jacob had already shown very good signs of becoming a top hand, and his boy was useful, trustworthy and ever willing to work. Even now as he thought of them he saw them coming from their soddy. They would share Christmas with them. This would be their first Christmas without wife and mother, and Carson was not going to allow them to suffer that loss alone at such a time.

Carson was doing well and enjoying his profession, and at thirty-five he just felt too young to give it all up and settle to the sameness of everyday chores and work habits. As he sat on the stoop that Christmas Eve, with his beloved girls kicking and struggling on a soft, buffalo calf robe at his feet, he heard his wife call that supper was ready. They had killed a fat hog at the first sign of snow, and the aroma was strong from the kitchen. Pork belly, spit roasted till crisp and delicious. Hominy grits[51] slathered with hog fat from the skillet, and a slice of cornpone to mop up the gravy, just like he remembered. Vegetables too were plentiful at this time of year and, all in all, he looked forward to the family feast he knew was now prepared.

Carson had brought a few bits and pieces from the Fort too. The cook's trimmings and offcuts from the buffalo, and some of the heavier leg bones for the marrow they contained. He would first warm the bones over a fire to soften the marrow, then break the bone, and spoon or scrape it out. When boiled and seasoned, the mixture would make a rich and nutritious stock for gravy, and, what was over and above the gravy needs, would end up as a stew when greens and vegetables were added. Nothing would be wasted, of that he was sure.

Carson did not believe anything should be wasted, for the Lord Himself had given instructions to gather up the fragments when He fed the five thousand. He must have had a plan for those twelve baskets of scraps. Someone somewhere must have been very glad of them, of that he was sure.

A few slices of buffalo hump, a tongue, with the heart and some liver, were likewise slung on his pack animal, for now and again Prairie Flower liked to cook those things she remembered from her tepee living, and Carson did not disappoint her.

Among other staples, Prairie Flower had in her root cellar the seasons harvest. Cobs of corn, potatoes, cabbages and onions. Peas and string beans, dried fruit, some peppers and squashes.[52] Blueberries, gathered in the fall before the bears, on their way to hibernation, got to the bramble patch, were an added treat. And a wedge of pumpkin pie, liberally sprinkled with sugared blueberries to finish off any meal, was an added item few men could refuse.

This life would be a satisfying prospect to any man, and Carson had a deep contentment in it, a feeling of wellbeing unsurpassed in all of life's pilgrimage. Sometimes, in moments like this, a verse of scripture would flit into his mind, and one did so now. He remembered old Grandma Turner using it to describe her life after young Carson had been brought to her. A gift from God, she said. *"Truly the lines are fallen to me in pleasant places."* What could be more pleasant he thought than a loving family and a horse ranch in Montana?

It was in that very moment, fleeting as it was, that he remembered so well, for the combination of his girls playing at his feet and the call for supper, almost settled his heart on staying. Almost, but not quite, for he shook off the strong pull of home life and decided there and then to continue as a scout, and a guide to the odd wagon train when an opportunity presented.

Also, since the Indians were making the noise of war, and there was tension in the air, he would give it a while longer!

# CHAPTER 16

Carson had camped at a cooling brook and had a fire going. He would take a break from the saddle and just relax in the shade an old and knarled oak provided. He had stopped here before, and to those who rode the trails, when a comfortable camp is found, it then becomes a welcome oasis whenever duty leads that way. Duty had done so today, and as he stretched contentedly against the mossy base of the tree, he savoured a cup of coffee while he chewed on a piece of jerky.[53] He was hungry, but more tired than hungry, and so, rather than cook up something, he chose the jerky. Prairie Flower and the girls had dried it, and with her own recipe had infused it with a delicious ingredient made from a mixture of crushed berries. Carson was all the happier to use it on that account. It was something from home, and he took comfort in having it. He missed his wife and girls when on the trail, and the jerky was a reminder of the intimacy between them.

Although he was happy with what life had brought him, there were dark and foreboding thoughts that kept his happiness from being complete.

It was the summer of 1876 and there was much unrest and national conflict. The newspapers kept the Fort up to date with news from back East, even though the railroad may have been a little late with it. It was not all good news either. The Nation was still busy with reconstruction, as the terrible aftermath of the Civil War was daily evidenced, but it would be a long hard road to healing.

In Carson's opinion, the day Lincoln was murdered, reconstruction lost its champion. Lincoln had been the wise man throughout all the events that led to and brought about the Civil War. He had not wanted war and had offered many an olive branch to the seceding States. It was they who opened hostilities by firing on Fort Sumter S.C. and, when the last shot marked the end of the slaughter four years later, 700,000 men lay dead. Such figures were hardly credible to the human mind, yet it was true, and the many cemeteries that were created to hold them were a constant reminder to succeeding generations of this reality.

Yet when Lincoln gave his address at Gettysburg, after the last and bloodiest battle of the war, he spoke not of Yankees or Rebels, or of defeat or victory, but he spoke eloquently of America, of unity, of the birth and founding just 87 years previously of a great nation, dedicated to the principle that all men are created equal.

Lincoln considered the Civil War as a test of that dedication, a proving of that principle, and wherein *all combatants* must share the honour of demonstrating that their great democracy, so recently born, *would* endure and *could* endure, even a struggle of such bloody and terrible carnage and loss. In considering the 50,000 men so recently fallen at Gettysburg, with the fallen of the other battles, he included them all as sharing in the same. There was no rhetoric of retaliation, revenge or retribution, and the speech only lasted two minutes!

While other blowhards and windbags went on for hours, the President of the United States finished in two minutes!

Yes, Carson thought, the country lost more than it realised when the cowards' bullet was fired that night in Ford's Theatre.

As he mulled over the past eleven years since the assassination, Carson could not fail to see the loss the whole country suffered as a consequence. The Black race did not yet enjoy the promises Lincolns Proclamation ought to have brought, for political decisions alone cannot change the hearts of men. Racial injustice was still rife in the Southern states, for there were those who would never give up the notion that *White is Might,* and the slain of the conflict only served to harden them in their twisted beliefs.

The Black man may have been legally free, but acceptance and equality comes at a much higher price! They were free to go, but *where* would they go? They were free to *do,* but *what* would they do? Oppression and dispossession were still their lot, and Carson wondered if it would ever be any different!

The words of old Zack often came to his mind when he thought of the day he first saw a black man. *"no civilised country could prosper for long with such cruel and unrighteous deeds allowed to continue among them".*

Here in the west, where Carson had made his home, there was trouble too. The frontier was a no man's land, where lawlessness prevailed at the point of a gun, and only those who were willing and courageous enough to meet force with force could establish peace and normality.

 On the Great Plains that same conflict was felt, as the ongoing Indian issue smouldered with an intensity that one day soon would explode in bloodshed and slaughter.

Carson was not blind to the situation going on around him. He had watched for years as the Indians had been betrayed, deceived and driven from their lands, all to make way for the greed of the prospector, the need of the settler, and the ongoing programme of governmental expansion.

Since the Fetterman disaster of 1866, Red Cloud had constantly harassed Forts Phil Kearney, FC Smith and Reno. These had been built to protect the flow of pioneers on their westward journey, and the miners on their way to the Montana goldfields. The continual raids, skirmishes and harassment of the army Forts, and on the increasing settler community, had led to loss of life, and had worn down the patience and resistance of both army and government administration.

The maintained Indian capability to strike at will, and with success too, brought an acceptance to all but the most hard-headed, that regular troops and cavalry, fighting by conventional means, were not capable of succeeding against such a foe. The cavalry and infantry were cumbersome in comparison to the fleet and agile Indian. Too slow to react, and unable to pursue, they fought a battle that became merely a military presence, a defending force without the capability of effective punitive measures, except when the Indian was snowbound in their winter camps, relatively helpless, and where their women and children presented an easy victory. Many good men and true found out too late that their experience in the Civil War was not to be compared to this new action. 'Set Piece' warfare, with its artillery barrages followed by the disastrous slow and orderly infantry advance on entrenched enemy lines, and cavalry charges on the same, had no bearing on the hit and run tactics of a foe who could outwit, outnumber and then outride the blue coated pony soldiers.

Carson often pitied the troopers tasked with this insurmountable problem. Often underfed, wearing ill-fitting uniforms and worn-out boots, riding horses that were, in many instances, in no shape to run, and living in unsanitary conditions that stank to high heaven in summer, they were not an army to instil fear into any opposing force, let alone those who had been brought to the point of outrage and revenge at the brutality and ill-treatment they had received over the years.

Carson noted that those Forts beyond the main supply line, or built in remote and isolated places, fared the worst when it came to resupply, for the pick of the provisions had already been taken, and very often those soldiers who needed it most went without.

Food was basic, often tasteless and most often in short supply. The army had what it called 'mainstays.' These 'mainstays' consisted of a menu of stew or hash, baked beans, hardtack,[54] salt, bacon, coarse bread, army contract range beef, sugar and molasses. Where a Fort was situated near a settlement it was possible to purchase or barter for fresh vegetables or fruit, eggs, chickens or such farmyard fare, but all too often this was only an empty concession, for the means whereby it could be implemented were not there. Carson got to know many of the soldiers over the years as he worked among them, and he also got to know what went on in the garrisons.

He was not listening therefore to idle tales when told the morale of the troopers was such as to make them a sadly ineffective fighting force. Men cannot fight well if they are not fed well. Living in squalid conditions year after year wore a man down. He missed his family, especially if he was married, and this gave rise to the oft-repeated phrase, *'Bachelors make the best soldiers'.*

The life of the soldier on the frontier was not to be envied, and those who sat in Washington and made decisions from the comfort of their lounges and smoking rooms would have been better employed had they made themselves acquainted with the realities of frontier peacekeeping.

Carson was no tactician, but common sense alone was enough for him to weigh up the situation, and he often wondered how long it would take for those in power to realise that pride and disdain are no substitute for a proper military strategy against a wily and elusive force of men who are willing to fight, not for wages, but simply for the right to live in peace, and sometimes for the right to live at all!

It had been this mounting Indian pressure on the War Department that forced the signing of the Fort Laramie Treaty, which Red Cloud of the Lakota signed in 1868. The treaty established sovereignty to the Great Sioux Nation of all South Dakota west of the Missouri River, including the Black Hills.

The Powder River country was to be ceded Indian Territory, as a hunting reserve for the Lakota, Cheyenne and Arapaho, of which country Red Cloud had expressly said,

*"No white person or persons shall be permitted to settle upon or occupy any portion, or without the consent of the Indians first being obtained to pass through."*

The treaty was clear enough in its wording, and the Indians accepted it, but Carson knew in his heart it would not last, and he had seen nothing in the previous years to cause him to think differently!

He would not have long to wait to find his thoughts materialise.

The ink had barely dried on the document when a rumour began that the Black Hills had gold! To settle the matter, in 1874 army superiors sent an officer on an expedition to investigate. It was a grand affair. Many men, wagons, supplies and provisions made the expedition a show of force, and it was not lost on the Indians! The Officer in charge had a glowing record of service in the Civil War, but a less than satisfactory record in his conduct, having been suspended for one year without pay for absenting himself without permission to go visit his wife!

His much-publicised success at Indian fighting was flawed also. Based as it was on a surprise raid on a Southern Cheyenne village six years earlier, when Black Kettles camp was destroyed, and men, women, children and older men bore the brunt of the camp raid, most of the warriors being elsewhere.

This raid, being the army's first victory over the Southern Plains tribes since the Civil War ended, was made much of on that account, and led to the officer being strengthened in his vain belief that he was fitted to deal with the Indian problem. It was indeed a foolish and ill-conceived opinion, both by the officer concerned and his superiors, and it was a sad day indeed for both army and Indians when George Armstrong Custer came to the Powder River country.

Flamboyant, and something of a dandy, (he was reported to perfume his long flowing locks) he and his wife Libbie formed a formidable team as far as self-promotion was concerned. He the Cavalier, riding in pursuit of fame and glory, her his Lady, supporting and encouraging him.

Custer's subsequent report on the Black Hills gold issue reflected his own character, exaggerated, overblown and dangerous. It was not long before the '68 Treaty was forgotten, as miners, prospectors and camp followers flocked to the gold fields like vultures to a carcass. Hide hunters came also, laying waste tons of buffalo meat simply for the hides that covered it!

It was all too much for the tribes to accept, and the breaking of the Treaty removed any chance there was for a bloodless outcome. The Powder River country became a gathering place for those willing to fight, and many came off the reservations to do so. The moving force behind this gathering was a spiritual leader of some note, a Hunkpapa Lakota, whose name was Sitting Bull.[55]

Sioux, Cheyenne and Arapaho had been gathering in many hundreds along the Little Bighorn, in the area between the tributary and the main river, and it was this growing encampment that the army, under the command of Brig. General Alfred H. Terry, descended upon in the form of three columns. He hoped by this three-pronged military strategy to prevent the escape of any fleeing Indians.

The newly formed 7th Cavalry made up the largest part of General Terry's command, and Custer, with his two hundred and ten strong columns, began confidently on what would be his last, and tragic, military engagement.

It was two days before a scouting party from General Terry's column came on the scene, and surveyed what could only be interpreted as an apparent rout and complete massacre of Custer's entire force. In one small area, horses and around 40 men were scattered about a grassy hill, Custer, two of his brothers, a nephew and brother-in-law among them! With 28 more bodies in a ravine 300 yards away. There had been no way to escape. The remainder of the slain force was scattered over an even wider area.

Many were reported to have killed themselves rather than be taken prisoner, and a bullet wound to the temple was a grim witness to this. The only sign of organised resistance was a few dead horses here and there forming apparent breastworks. The bodies of the troopers were stripped and traditionally mutilated, as was Custer's.

Carson heard all these things with sadness. First Fetterman, now Custer. Both rash, brash and arrogant when it came to recognising the Indians capability, and both having a greatly exaggerated view of their own and the US Cavalry's ability when it came to fighting them. There were no white witnesses to Custer's disastrous engagement, but scouts who brought him intelligence reports before departing to seek the other units in the field, told it all.

The massacre had not taken place without strategic errors and fatal assumptions. Even though his scouts had told him it was the biggest Indian camp they had ever seen, Custer did not deviate from his planned course of action, not even to investigate the accuracy of the report!

Custer's attack was hurried, and engaged upon a day earlier than planned because of a fear of the Indian camp being alerted and scattering. There was more concern of Indians escaping, than in any numerical disadvantage or danger his force might encounter!

After it was all over the military commanders made the best of it, saying it was an utterly incomprehensible decision. Carson thought another word might have been better employed, for in his mind it was unforgivable!

Instead of a sleeping camp, Custer rode into an angry mass of warriors, up to 2,000 strong, prepared to fight, and much better armed than many of his troopers.

Those on the Indian side told of the swiftness of the massacre. That it was over *"in the length of time it takes a man to eat a meal."*

While the Sioux celebrated the victory, and the army mourned the loss of its men, it would prove a turning point in the struggle. The Indian victory would be short-lived, for courage alone is never enough for nomadic peoples to win wars against the might and resources of a federal government. When at last the realisation of what was needed set in, the War Department awoke to its task.

After Custer's defeat, Brig. General George Crook and Brig. General Alfred H. Terry remained immobile for seven weeks until they had amassed a 2,000-strong force, and in August took the field again against the hostiles.

The lesson had been learned Carson thought wryly, but the tragic human cost involved removed any satisfaction he may have gained from it.

The following year, on May 7, 1877, General Nelson A. Miles, now in command, fought the last battle with a remaining band of hostiles.

Sitting Bull escaped to Canada, Crazy Horse had  surrendered, and the widows and orphans on both sides were left with their grief and their memories. The Great Sioux War was over!

It had been a year of unimaginable suffering, upheaval and loss for a people whose only desire was to live peaceably with the open plains as their heritage, and the buffalo as their means of provision. Beyond that, they had asked nothing of the white man. But it was not to be.

Carson thought it a pity that gold should be the reason for such a great injustice, and that land greed should take the place of human compassion in the hearts of the nation. He had seen it in individuals throughout his life, but to see it come to life in actual governmental policy was something else again. He was glad he had no part in it.

# CHAPTER 17

Carson knew something was wrong when he saw the letter. It was in Grandma Turner's tiny and sloping scribble, and the envelope was well filled. He had just picked it up at the livery stable, where old Mose Harper eked out a living from tending, stabling, sometimes shoeing horses, and harness mending.

Carson had an arrangement with Mose, whereby any traveller going East would drop Carson's mail from the Turners, and Carson in turn would send his to the storekeeper at Twin Forks by the same method. The arrangement worked well, if sometimes a little slow, but no one minded that out here. A letter was a letter, slow or not.

He motioned to Mose that he needed to read this letter, and Mose nodded to his office, which was an empty stall at the rear of the livery. It contained a single chair, and a short length of lumber resting on two kegs served as a table for any note Mose needed to take.

Carson drew up the chair and opened the envelope. There were several pages in Grandma Turner's hand, and he read them through slowly, some of them a second time.

Zack was dead. The letter was a month old, but no matter. Carson was very glad that Grandma Turner had been wise enough and understanding enough to give him all the news she could of his death. She knew it would give Carson peace of heart to know these things, and that although not being there in person, he would have in his mind a picture of his father's last moments, and take comfort from that knowledge.

Zack had been killed. It was not an unusual death in the mountainous country where it had happened, but it was unfortunate nevertheless, in that perhaps it may have been prevented.

The incident had taken place on 'Old Ned,'[56] the last mountain on the descent from the Musselshell.[57] The mountain got its name from an ancient prospector who spent a lifetime looking for the mother lode he always claimed was there. One day, long before Carson's time, Ned came whoopin' and hollerin' into town claiming he had hit pay dirt at last. He had told them it was there and now he had the proof. Flashing around a fistful of large nuggets, Ned bought some needed supplies and headed back to his diggings. He was never seen again. He just disappeared. Folks noticed that another man left town the very same day, and he was never seen again either. A half-breed called 'Hogpen', on account of his dirty and unkempt appearance.

Too shiftless to work, and too lazy to wash, some good solid church going people were willing to swear that if you were downwind of Hogpen you could smell him at a hundred yards. Some were willing to stretch it further, but a hundred yards seemed to be the general opinion.

The story was that Hogpen had followed Ned to his claim, murdered him, and took off with whatever Ned had already extracted from his mine. Carson was familiar with the mountain, and the history too, for it was Zack who had told him the story. Zack and Carson had made camp years ago at the very place where Zack was killed, for it had become Zack's habit to overnight at that spot rather than risk the mountain trail in the darkness.

There was forage and shelter for the horses, and a spring-fed trickle of good water filled a sizable rock depression before overflowing into the greenery surrounding it. Camp sites like this were not easily found on the trail, and to men like Zack they became a focal point, a place to arrive before darkness, a place akin to home for a weary traveller.

Zack had insisted on holding revival meetings for a little group of settlers high up in the hills. He had promised Grandma Turner that it would be his last circuit, and she good naturedly gave in to his enthusiasm. The Circuits were his very life, and she knew that, so even though he was well above 70, she would not discourage him. The full story came from two trappers who were not far away at their cabin, making ready for the new season.

They had heard two shots late one afternoon and thought someone was hunting their trap line area. The trail had its own stern code, and everyone knew it, and as hunting another's area was akin to stealing, the trappers set out to find the poachers. They soon picked up the smell of wood smoke and followed it to its source. On reaching Zack's camp they found his fire with his evening meal sitting uneaten beside it.

Thirty yards away two horses were hobbled on a loose running line to allow them to graze. Both Zack's saddle and pack saddle were laid against a large fir root and covered with a small piece of tarp against the evening dew, for this high up the night dew could be heavy. Nothing was touched or moved. The camp was neat and peaceful looking. The horses however were skittish, whinnying quietly and constantly, showing the whites of their eyes, and pulling away from the camp as far as the running line would allow.

The trappers waited a moment or two, taking all this in, watching from the shelter of the tree line, not wanting to be surprised by a hostile reception, and thus make a bad situation become worse for them. It was in these moments of silent observation that they saw it.

A large grizzly lay face down in the scrub close to the horses. It was a huge animal, light in colour, which was why they did not immediately see it in the brush.

Moving forward slowly they approached the scene, and to the horror of both they saw an arm, with a pistol still in the hand, protruding from under the great bulk of the bear. As Carson read Grandma Turner's scribble he might as well have been there, for his mind's eye could see and understand every scene thus described.

The trappers, after making sure the bear was dead, rolled it off old Zack. He had been killed instantly, for the charging bear, in its dying moment, had reached him, and a last mighty swipe of its paw had crushed the old man's skull like an eggshell.

Over from Zack's body lay his rifle, it had been fired recently, and the smell was still strong from the muzzle. The pistol too had been fired, and when they skinned the bear, they saw where two bullets had struck the animal in the heart region, with only the width of a hand between them.

The picture was now clear to the trappers. Zack had been at his supper when the grizzly had spooked the horses. He had gone to scare it off and it had charged him. Firing his rifle first he then cast it aside and drew and fired his pistol, but it was too late for both such weapons. Both shots would have been killing shots in a hunting situation, but a close-quarter charge by an enraged animal of this size was an entirely different situation.

Although a heart shot will always bring a beast down, sometimes it takes some seconds, and sometimes only after a short run. A hunter at a distance can afford those seconds, and even a short run, but a charging animal, just feet away, and fast closing with every breath, may not be stopped in time. It was common knowledge in the mountains, and Carson always obeyed it, that you don't shoot a large calibre animal with a small calibre bullet, even a heart shot!

Carson regretted now he did not press old Zack harder to change his rifle and calibre. But Zack was a preacher, not a hunter. His thoughts did not run on the needs of heavier weaponry, or of any real danger from bears or cougar. He kept to the trail mostly, and was content to follow his time-worn habit, trusting in God to protect him. Zack was a trusting man. If he did not disturb them he thought, they would not disturb him. Such was Carson's love for the old man that even in his thoughts he shrank from criticism of him, but he did allow himself to consider the possibility, that had Zack changed from flint and powder to cartridge, even in .44 calibre, it would not have significantly threatened the old man's strong belief in the providence of God. And he may still be alive today!

Grandma Turner's letter ended by telling of how the trappers buried Zack where he fell, and built a large mound of stones and boulders over the grave. They did not know the old preacher, but they had heard of him over the years, and his mode of dress when they found him confirmed his identity to them. Black tailcoat and knee breeches, clean white shirt with two white frontal bibs, they didn't need school larnin' to recognise the livery of the circuit riding preacher, and Zack always took great pride in his presentation as a servant of the King. The horses and his belongings they returned to her, in an act of great kindness and thoughtfulness.

Carson's eyes moistened as he read the description the trappers gave to Grandma Turner. How he loved the old man. How Zack not only *looked* the part but *was* the part. Carson knew many who took the place of evangelists and disciples, and they were but 14 karat sharpies. But old Zack was different. Through and through he was solid gold, and died strong in the faith he had professed so earnestly.

Even in the very face of death he did not flinch, for throughout all his life *'he looked for a city,'* and when his call came he was not afraid to go. Not to the very last second, for the powder burn from his pistol on the fur of the bear said it all. Carson had long wanted the old couple to come and live with him, now it would only be Grandma, and he would welcome her, and so would Prairie Flower and the girls. Carson could think of no better schoolin' for them than to listen to Grandma Turner as she took them under her wing and into her heart, even as she did to him so many years ago.

# CHAPTER 18

I f Carson ever regretted the few extra years he spent working for the army, and he did so at times, he was to change his mind through a most remarkable incident, and one which brought his army scouting career to a close with a sense of lasting peace and contentment.

But all that was in the future. In the next few years, he would witness what would become the final destruction of the great buffalo herds. A railroad engineer once told him that on one occasion he had to bring his train to a halt to allow a buffalo herd to pass. It took nine hours [58] for the black mass of docile beasts to clear the line. Almost stretching to the horizon, the great sea of animals moved northwards on their autumn migration.

Not anymore, thought Carson, as he recalled the engineer's words. The army's high command, and the thoughtless indifference of the public at large, obsessed as they were for western progress, had signed the death warrant for these Great Plains herds, and at the same time entirely removed all hope the Indians had for their centuries-old nomadic existence.

Carson could never quite understand how a civilised nation could so wantonly pursue such a course, but pursue it they did, and what he had seen with his own eyes confirmed it without question. The buffalo hunters were legion. Killing, skinning, and stacking, the huge piles of hides were later lifted by other wagons and drawn to the nearest railhead.

Buffalo fever had gripped the nation. Hides were needed back east for industry, and all else was swallowed up in the rush to attain them. There were no limits to the killing. Everyone involved was convinced that as long as there was a buffalo left standing, the Indians would never settle on a reservation!

Oh, it was never written down, it was never a printed policy, either from the army or the government, but it was there just the same. Cruel, methodical, immoral and wasteful, it was promoted and encouraged on a large scale, and none were more destructive in pursuing it than the US Army.

One day Carson was returning to his scouting responsibilities after a month on his ranch when he first heard the cannon. Again and again, the big gun roared, so much so that he began to think that the Fort was in peril, and under attack. But even as he thought so his reason told him it could not be. No man alive knew these hills and plains as he did, and he knew that there were not enough Indians within a hundred miles to cause such an alarm. Perhaps it was a celebration. Maybe an artillery drill!

In times of relative peace, soldiers needed something to make the boredom of compound life bearable, and very often the commander, if he was wise, thought on these things and sought to bring some distraction, some interest to the troopers by way of such activities. Carson still had ten miles to travel, and as he rode the methodical boom of the artillery piece continually broke the silence.

When at last he came into view of the army post nothing could have prepared him for the sight that met his eyes. A great herd of plains buffalo had ambled past the Fort on their migration trail, and had it surrounded. To clear the Fort area and its surrounding corrals, the cannon had been used, and great piles of dead and dying beasts lay all around, score upon score of them. The action had little effect. The herd continued on their trek, quite oblivious to the slaughter among them.

The next few days however revealed the folly of the cannonades. The overpowering stench of the rotting carcasses almost drove the soldiers from their barracks, and a detail had to be ordered to clear the mounds of carnage, first dragging them downwind of the Fort and then burning them. To Carson this was incomprehensible waste and slaughter. It was not a secret either. There was no shame in these acts of barbarism, and buffalo killing had become a very attractive commodity for the US government, a sport offered to those it wanted to draw into closer economic, social, and perhaps even military association. Carson often cast his mind back to the growing list of events that he alone could remember.

Why else would a Duke of Russia[59] be invited to come with his whole entourage and engage in indiscriminate and wanton slaughter of beasts that were so precious to the Indian, yet so harmless to man? Using army rifles and army ammunition, with army guides and escort, they shot hundreds, only to let them lie and rot on the plain. Contests were engaged in to see who could bring in the most buffalo tongues for special occasions at the garrison. Wagons would be allocated to teams of hunters who would cut the tongues from their kills, and leave the carcasses to rot. Nearly one ton of meat sacrificed for the sake of a tongue weighing at the most two pounds!

He had watched the situation worsen steadily over the years, but now it had become an acceptable sideshow against the boredom of the frontier, and for those whose lives were otherwise fruitless and unexciting.

Dandies, dudes, politicians, senators, English aristocrats, noblemen from Europe, and businessmen from the East were likewise being treated to this 'exciting sport' as it was billed, although the skills required to participate were minimal, and bore no resemblance to actual hunting. The buffalo's docile nature, plus the vast numbers in the slow-moving herds, told against them, and anyone who could be guided to a herd and point a rifle, could hardly fail to bring an animal down. Carson was not a lettered man, but it needed not letters to recognise how shallow and superficial politicians and dignitaries really were when they were so easily bought over with a stage-managed buffalo hunt, a whiskey before dinner, and a buffalo tongue delicacy included in the menu!

It pained him to see these things, and to see his nation's leaders engaging in such tacky and cheap behaviour. Carson had no time for such. Frivolous in matters that were the very foundation of his Christian upbringing, callous in their disdain for the Indians and their way of life, and wantonly destructive of a national resource that, as far as Carson knew, no other nation had, he loathed these opportunists, and when they were around the Fort he avoided them.

Carson had not yet participated in any of these army-sanctioned buffalo killings or feastings. He always made it his aim to be otherwise occupied when such was being planned, but he knew he could not maintain a policy of abstentionism, and sooner or later he must make a choice.

Nothing stays the same for long he thought, and in his heart his time on the trail was coming to a close. He was saddened that, given the courage and sacrifice of the early settlers, heading west with everything they owned in a wagon, spending months on a trek of thousands of miles, and their wake dotted with the lonely graves of loved ones as a testimony of their endeavour, that the land they had already conquered behind them was already being exploited and pillaged by those intent on enriching themselves at all costs, whether in the natural resources of the land, the great beasts that roamed it, or the Indians, whose very existence was a daily challenge to their selfish and cruel purposes. Carson wanted no part of it, and his heart told him so daily!

It was in this frame of mind that he found himself one morning in an army court, the commanding officer presiding.

# CHAPTER 19

Awood detail had been attacked and two draught horses were stolen just a few days before. Hearing rifle fire another detail was sent to assist them, but it was not an attack on the detail. A few young Indians had merely knocked a guard senseless and ran off with a team, which had been unhitched and taken to some shade trees to wait for the return journey.

It was not long before a search party brought in three Indians, bound hand and foot to their ponies. A Crow scout had led the search party, and three Arapaho had been arrested and brought in. When Carson heard of it he smiled wryly to himself. A Crow scout finds three Arapaho! Everyone looks after their own he thought, even if it means the death sentence to those wrongfully arrested.

No one was killed in the incident with the horses, but these Indians would hang just the same. Indeed, their guilt or innocence mattered not. They were Indians, horses had been stolen, and in such circumstances, they would be held as hostages, one hanged each day until the real culprits came in and gave themselves up. It was hardly justice, but the practice prevailed, for both the Indian and the buffalo were marked for destruction!

It was not Carson's business however, but he had his own opinion just the same, as he had on most things. Injustice was something he detested above all else, and injustice awaited these three today, and a rope would complete it tomorrow!

Carson had a long ride ahead of him and was making ready when he heard the call to bring the three Indians from the guardhouse. Another minute and he would have been gone!

"Sergeant, bring Spotted Tail, Running Bear, Great Elk".

Carson froze. The cinch strap fell from his fingers as his hand lost its hold, and the hair stood on the nape of his neck. In a few fleeting moments he was back under the tree, and his childhood friend tumbling from its branches. Could this be him? Could this really be *that* Great Elk? He lifted his eyes above the saddle horn and fixed them on the guardhouse door. Three Indians were brought out one by one and began the walk across the courtyard.

Although the distance was not far, Carson could not discern anything that his memory retained of his childhood friend, but he noted they were of an age that fitted the time scale, and one of them walked with a limp!

He was now in a quandary. He had work to do. A wagon train had been left without a guide, and had to be met near Fort Laramie and led further west before the snows brought all to a standstill. Many people were depending on him, and that burden was heavy on his shoulders. But now he had a matter of life and death to deal with, if indeed his hunch or suspicion was true concerning Great Elk. One thing was sure however, after hearing the name called out, and knowing the consequences for the three unfortunates, he could not simply ride off as if he had not heard. It did not take Carson long to decide.

Larsen would go to Fort Laramie. Larson, or 'The Swede' as he was more generally known, was a little older than himself and had spent his life in these parts. No one knew the trails and water holes better than Larsen. He would be glad of the work, for he was recovering from a bad break in his left leg and had lost much work as a consequence. Scribbling a quick note for Larsen, and sending it to the Sutler's store, he had no regrets as to his choice. The settlers would be in safe hands with 'The Swede'.

Unsaddling his horse, and unloading again his pack animal, he made his way to the officer's mess where the court was being held.

It was one of the better buildings within the compound. Built of logs, notched and caulked neatly, it had a spacious interior that doubled for many events that called for space and comfort. Anniversaries, Christmas celebrations, the yearly officer's ball.

The prisoners sat at the front facing the table where the commanding officer and his jury sat. Colonel Archibald McBride, a man in his sixties, was looked upon as a fair man in his running of the Forts affairs. Married, but with no children, he spent a lot of his time in his own quarters, and could be seen walking the inside perimeter in the cool of the evening with his wife Martha. She was a homely lady, and was looked upon by the other wives as a motherly figure. Always ready to help and assist in times of need. Carson thought that if he ever had the misfortune to be before someone in a trial, he could do a lot worse than have Colonel McBride as his judge. But the Colonel had only one vote, that was the problem, and the others he had picked did not share McBride's kindly demeanour.

The Colonel had been limited in his choice, for there was only room for so many officers in an outpost of two hundred troopers, and he had picked seven all told, but it was enough. A decision would not take long considering the charges to be brought, and whoever he would have picked would not have increased his chances of an acquittal.

Behind the prisoners sat a motley assortment of hangers-on and camp followers. The usual loungers and scroungers were there of course, they never missed. Such proceedings were a welcome distraction to the idle boredom they endured daily. Half a dozen settlers, who had come to the Sutler's store that morning were also there, as were a few of the local 'friendlies' from those tribes who did business with the army. There were not above twenty persons in all, but enough to witness the way in which the prisoners would be tried, and enough to carry the news far afield in the event of any blatant wrongdoing!

In any event the proceedings followed a general order, court protocols were adhered to, again generally, and it was a regular 'set piece' trial. A young lieutenant had been appointed for prosecution, Kirby by name, and another was given the task of defence. Carson found a chair at the back of the room and was just in time to hear the charges being presented to the Court. It was not a complicated case, and each item of evidence was read out one by one.

- Horses had been stolen from a wood detail on October 3, 1880. A trooper had been badly injured in the process.
- Five Indians had been seen in the vicinity just before the crime.
- They all rode paint ponies.[60]
- In a follow-up search these three Indians had been found in a gully, just five miles from the scene. They all had paint ponies.

After outlining the above the young lieutenant then went on in a passionate tirade that was designed to curry favour with the general opinion held by those sitting in judgement.

"It is our case that these three were of the five thieves that day, and had already sent two of their number on with the horses. Not expecting a search party, they had brazenly lit a fire and remained to eat not far from the scene where the crime was committed.

I put this before the court today as a very serious offence. The young trooper guarding the horses could have been killed. For all these savages knew he might have been left for dead. He is still off duty due to his injuries. This nuisance raiding and stealing has got out of hand, and this outpost has had enough of it. Young men, good men and true, are hazarding their lives daily to make safe the frontier, to build a nation, to forge a future for our children and grandchildren out of a harsh and forbidding landscape.

Leaving behind wife and children, they endure the loneliness, dangers and rigors of military life uncomplainingly and compassionately, and not only deserve to be protected, but allowed to go about mundane yet crucial duties such as water and wood details without looking over their shoulder lest native treachery bring death or destruction to them, or their mounts taken by unwashed parasites, whose only aim in life it seems is to live off other people's hard won endeavour, while they breed another generation of the same.

I am asking that this behaviour be stopped this very day. That we use our God given responsibility to ensure that this be so. Christianity and thievery cannot go hand in hand. Those of us who have had the privilege of a Christian upbringing, who have been taught right from wrong, who have sacrificed so much to serve our nation among these ignorant savages, and who have witnessed so much of their savagery on decent settler folk, and indeed on our own brave US Cavalry, must now take on the responsibility to do our utmost to bring Christianity to them in a more tangible way than before.

It is our bounden duty to do so. We cannot shirk our Christian responsibilities in this. We must show them that if they do not heed the evident lessons and benefits of civilisation we have brought to them, they must bear the penalty for their wilful obstinacy. It is my proposal therefore that this court make an example of these three thieves by imposing the death penalty.

The Indians in these parts who are causing so much unnecessary grief and hardship must be made to see that the price of horses is now being raised, and those who embark on such activity will now pay with their life."

Carson sat silently and listened to this overblown and exaggerated characterisation of the US Cavalry, and thought to himself that in all his years he had never encountered the lieutenant's idealistic description, and neither had anyone else as far as he was concerned. The prosecutions references to Christianity led him to wonder what branch of 'Christianity' he was extolling, for it was in direct contradiction to what old Grandma Turner had instilled into him from an early age.

The attack on the Indians status in the human race, "ignorant savages", "unwashed parasites" Carson thought would go down well with those who sat in judgement, nodding their heads wisely every now and then as Kirby waxed eloquent in his tirade.

This man was out for blood, and for the first time Carson felt deep within himself that he had made the right decision to attend this court. He may not be able to change the outcome, but at least he could try. And that to him was the only badge of honour worth wearing.

His belief in 'always trying' was found in a verse old Grandma Turner had taught him,

*"To him that knoweth to do good, and doeth it not, to him it is sin".*

Sinning by silence was therefore not an option for the frontiersman. He had lived his life by the precepts taught from the Good Book, and he was not about to forsake them now, and certainly not for Kirby. As Kirby took his seat and the defence rose for rebuttal, Colonel McBride intervened. "Mr Kirby, do you wish to call any witnesses that may have a bearing on the charges outlined".

"Thank you, Colonel, but no witnesses are needed in this case, for the case speaks for itself. There is nothing to be gained by wasting the courts time going through protocols that are so obviously unnecessary".

"Very well Mr Kirby, as you wish, but I felt it necessary to give you the opportunity. I call the defence".

The defence was likewise a young man, fresh out of West Point. Tall and well groomed, dark neatly trimmed sideburns set off an image of a man who would not scruple to defend what he believed in life, regardless of the opposition.

He had been spoken against behind his back since he first arrived, for jealously was rampant among the officers and enlisted men. Having graduated with honours from the Academy, and with letters of commendation signed by those who mattered in the affairs of men, Lieutenant Ruben J. Cogburn was his own man.

He did not accept the 'whites only' programme that was deeply entrenched within all society here on the frontier, and nowhere more so than in the US Army. He was known for his powers of reasoning, insight and fairness, and was not afraid to let his opinions be known, including those concerning the Indian.

This rankled with his superiors somewhat, as men with little personal gift in speaking their mind are wont to be envious against those whose achievements are greater than their own, and whose independence was a constant reminder of their own inadequacy's. But Cogburn always knew his own limitations whatever the cause, and knowing so he was not about to give up lightly where he found the cause worthy of an honest challenge.

Unlike Kirby before him, he did not immediately rush into his strategy. He stood up slowly, tall and imposing, looking first at the prisoners and then at the commanding officer and his men. A long look at the paper he held in his hand completed his silent opening enactment, and when he spoke all ears were listening, and all eyes fastened upon him, Carson's in particular.

"Gentlemen, I have listened with great attention to Mr Kirby's charges against these men, and with which he hopes to bring a death sentence upon them. With all due respect to my fellow officer, from a legal perspective alone I must point out the utter folly of such a proposal.

Leaving aside for the moment the racial slurs contained in the prosecution's case, which are not evidence by the way, and dealing solely with the facts of the matter, please allow me to point out some areas of highly questionable validity to say the least.

On October 3, 1880, just three days ago, two draught horses were stolen from a wood detail, and a trooper received a head wound in the crime. Five Indians were seen in the vicinity at that time, all riding paint ponies!

My first question is gentlemen, how many other Indians were also seen by the wood detail that day? Is it not true that there are 'friendlies' in the vicinity of this outpost constantly, those who have accepted the fact of reservation life, and those who seek to continue a peaceful working co-existence with the settlers, and to live out their lives in the hope that the future will bring better things for them?

These can be seen daily; they have become a common sight. How far could we ride without seeing the Indian on our journey? Unlike my colleague Mr Kirby, I have spoken to those soldiers involved in this incident, and Sergeant Meyers, who led that wood detail, tells me that they saw many Indians that day, some larger and some smaller groups.

Gentlemen, the fact that five Indians were seen in the vicinity before this crime was committed is bereft of credibility, and utterly devoid of serious consideration when we think of the circumstances surrounding this Fort and the peaceful nature of the Indians hereabouts.

The fact that they were said to be riding paint ponies is likewise bereft of any usefulness to this Court. Let me ask you gentlemen another question, that must be answered from the heart. When last did you see an Indian riding *any other* than a paint pony? How many bays, how many sorrels, how many chestnuts, buckskins or appaloosa have you noticed with an Indian astride it?

To say five Indians were riding paint ponies is like stating they all had arms and legs! Gentlemen, I appeal to your common sense and reason, and your unbiased opinion of the so-called evidence my fellow soldier has introduced. It is not evidence, it is commonplace!

Again a question.

Are three Indians found roasting a prairie chicken to be arrested as horse thieves just because they are within riding distance of a crime?

Really gentlemen, can we be so naive as to consider these men as the culprits?

I have spoken at length to trooper O'Reilly, the injured man, and he assures me that the men who attacked him were all young bucks, excitable, inexperienced and not above eighteen years old. He was only overpowered because of the sheer weight of numbers. They did not kill him nor steal his rifle or sidearm, and although he was injured, he is thankful that they spared his life, and he is of the opinion that they had no intention of murder, but were just a few young bucks on a mischievous spree. One of them even lost his arrows and quiver in the melee, and they are unmistakably Crow. I have the quiver and arrows in court, for any who wish to consider real evidence, retrieved from the scene!

None of these prisoners fit the description given by trooper O'Reilly. These are all mature men who offered no resistance whatsoever to the party who arrested them. Gentlemen, it is not a crime for men to enjoy a day's hunting together, or to roast a prairie chicken over a camp fire. Captain Fraser, who led the search party, saw evidence of a small camp. These men had been in that gully for a few days at least, and the captain was surprised when the Crow scout named them as the horse thieves.

As far as the description of their character and persons is concerned, as being unwashed savages and idle parasites, there are many white men within the vicinity of this Fort who may beg to differ with this unkind designation were it put to them concerning their wives, who are Indian wives I may add. I am quite sure that Mr Bridger would not acquiesce to Mr Kirby's opinion, and perhaps may put his opinion a little stronger and in a more physical manner than this court allows!

Gentlemen, we are on dangerous ground indeed when we accept racial discrimination, slander and personal animosity as being tenets of the Christian faith. As far as I am aware God wrote only one Bible, and in my reading of it I never once came across such acrimony taught as my colleague has just evidenced.

I am not a student of theology, far from it in fact, but what I do know of Christianity tells me that *mercy and truth* alone must pervade and undergird our every word and deed. We will all be judged on that. Gods Truth from a heart of truth must be our watchword in all our dealings with our fellow man, and if those fellow men have not yet attained to our social privileges, or the blessings brought to us through civilised development, or indeed the spiritual comforts of the gospel of Christ, then hanging them will not help our cause, or make our message a more attractive one to accept.

Sirs, officers and gentlemen, I implore you in the name of all that is holy and good, release these men".

It was indeed a spirited speech, and the earnestness of the heart from whence it came could not be hidden.

As Lieutenant Cogburn took his seat the Court was hushed and still. Even the most hard bitten of the gathered company were silenced. The commanding officer looked on the scene with a gaze that bespoke a man touched and moved by what he had just heard. Perhaps Cogburn's words had revived an old memory for him, something perhaps that somehow, somewhere had been lost along the way. Whatever it was it remained a secret, for McBride's attention was just then taken by the officer on his right, and the moment was gone.

There was an intense exchange among those seven men for long minutes, attended with much gesticulating, hand movement, stern looks and pointing at legal papers, and Carson knew it did not bode well for the prisoners. At last the Colonel called the Court to order and a silent expectancy fell on the proceedings.

"Gentlemen, a majority of my colleagues are of the opinion that these men are guilty, and must face the hangman. However, I am not entirely satisfied that these charges can be sustained, and so before final judgement is given I am going to give opportunity to the prisoners to speak for themselves. It cannot be that we hang a man without giving him the opportunity to speak. Surely we owe that much to any man.

I call on Sergeant Quinncannon to act as interpreter, as I know he has a good grasp of the Arapaho language, and I appoint Great Elk here to be spokesman for the three. Let's hear what they have to say before we move on any further."

Quinncannon, a great hulk of an Irishman, Master of Horse to the company, stepped forward to where the prisoners sat and stood before Great Elk. Carson's gaze was riveted to what was going on just thirty feet beyond him. He did not want to miss a word.

The Colonel spoke again. "Sergeant, just give it as it comes, as if it comes from yourself. No need for 'he said', 'they said' or any explanations of that sort, and Sergeant, I want no holding back in deference to any officer here, we understand you are only the interpreter, so don't mince your words on account of us".

# CHAPTER 20

uinncannon stepped closer to Great Elk and spoke quietly to him, no doubt explaining what was required and how he wanted him to speak.

Carson knew that this Great Elk, if he indeed was his boyhood companion, must have at least a smattering of English, and very possibly good English, for the Indians had an ear for languages, but in providing an interpreter for him the Colonel was giving him the best opportunity he could in very trying circumstances.

Frontier life was sometimes very difficult, and especially for those now in the Colonel's position, where a decision may have to be made that breaks the normal routine, and appears to give sympathy to the Indian. Reputations and careers had been lost by many through the same, and no one knew that better than the Colonel. One wrong move and this could go all the way to Washington, and the Colonel's experience told him that there were plenty sitting alongside him who would not scruple to make such a complaint. Kirby was livid that his own passionate theatricals had not worked, and there were others likeminded the Colonel was sure.

Great Elk stood and faced the seven men in whose hands his life now lay.

"I am Great Elk, son of chief Many Horses, my grandfather was Wolf -Man, a mighty and wise counsellor to our people, and whose name still lives on today in the mountains far west of here. When I speak I do so for my ancestors, myself and my fellow tribesmen. Before the white men came we had the prairie as our hunting ground, and the buffalo to provide us with warm tepees, robes against the cold of winter, and meat for our children.

We had everything we wanted and needed from this land that the Great Spirit had given us. We were a happy people, and our children grew up not knowing the word fear. We slept well in those times. Our womenfolk were safe, and our children had the prairie to roam in. Then the white man came, and the happiness we once knew never came to us again.

We watched as the white man destroyed and wasted everything that we honoured and valued. Our land was taken, our buffalo were slaughtered only for their hides, and our people were killed to make way for these people who come in many wagons from where the sun rises each day. We saw all this and were sad.

When we killed a buffalo it was because we were hungry, or our children were cold and needed a warm robe to sleep in. But for the white man to kill just to make them happy, and to leave the meat for the coyote and eagle, this we could not understand.

We believed the messages and treaties sent to us from the Great Father in Washington. That he would give us lands for ourselves and our little ones. That we could have our own hunting grounds where no white man could waste or destroy, and where the buffalo would be plentiful for all our needs.

Yes, we believed him, but his promises were all false. The treaties were broken and our lands taken again and again. When we called a War Council, my grandfather Wolf Man said no, for we could not win this battle against the blue coated soldiers, and if we fought them many lodges would be without fathers and husbands, and many children would be hungry. When my grandfather died, my father, chief Many Horses, even though he knew we were being deceived, never took to the battlefield against the white man or his pony soldiers, for he remembered the words of his father. He always hoped that the future would bring a lasting peace, but he died believing in an empty hope, for it has not done so.

Even to this day our band has not yet risen against the white man and his plans to take this land from us. Even I, Great Elk, although my wife was murdered by Fetterman, and my first child stolen by him, have never called a council of war or gathered my people to battle.

Now you take me and my friends from a peaceful hunting party and accuse us of stealing your horses. You are going to hang us, not because we stole horses, but because we are Indians. Is this the way of the Great Father in Washington? Will we now die in a place we thought as safe. Will our friendship mean nothing to you? Must I die like my father, with a heart sorrowing for the wrongs done to us, and broken promises as many as the dried leaves on the prairie?

Great Elk has spoken"

Taking the Court by surprise Kirby sprang to his feet. "Colonel, I must protest in the strongest possible terms that a savage can come here and besmirch the good name and reputation of Captain Fetterman".

"Sit down Mr Kirby." "Colonel, this is a travesty…. "Sit down Mr Kirby or I will have you in contempt. You have had your say. It is now this man's right to have his say. If you wish to cross question him when he has finished you have a right to do so, but I remind you it will be done according to the dictates and protocols of the Court. The Colonel turned his gaze to his Sergeant. "Sergeant, ask Great Elk to tell us more of that Fetterman story."

Quinncannon again went forward to Great Elk, and once again the accused took up his role as spokesman and continued.

"Many moons ago, in the time of the falling leaves, my wife was in camp making pemmican for the coming winter snows. Many other wives were there also, for the young men were on the great hunt before winter. My wife had her uncle with her, an old man, and her younger brother. They were there to help, for she was near to give birth. Her younger brother had gone to a nearby forest to gather firewood when he saw the pony soldiers attack the camp.

He was very near to them but he could do nothing, being but a child. He saw the soldiers kill all the people with their long knives and pistols, riding over and through the tepees and destroying the food they had prepared. My wife's uncle brought down a horse with a lance before he was cut to pieces, some soldiers dismounting to join in the cutting and slashing.

When the soldiers rode away the boy caught a pony that had survived and brought me word.

I saw with my own eyes the iron hoof prints of the soldier's horse who had ridden into my wife's tepee and murdered her, shot through the heart, and my new born papoose was gone. It had not yet sucked her breast, but it was gone. Now I too will soon be gone, for the pony soldiers will not be satisfied until we are all gone.

Colonel McBride turned to Kirby. "Mr Kirby?"

Kirby rose slowly. He had been twice bested publicly on account of this Indian, and he did not want a repeat, so he gathered his wits together and thought that the least said now the better.

"Sirs. I have listened to this witness tell a tale which is preposterous, to say the least. A tale almost twenty years old, and which is now long consigned to history. This story lays a very serious charge against a brave colleague and soldier, who gave his own life in defence of this nation, and is no longer here to answer for himself.

However, being a fair-minded man, and desirous to see a just outcome in this sad and sorry case, I propose this to you. If a credible witness can verify this story, or confirm this character defamation of Captain Fetterman, just one credible witness gentlemen, is that too much to ask, and I will withdraw all charges. I cannot be fairer than that.

Kirby sat down, confident that he had delivered the death sentence. Where would this Indian go with the proposal he had just made? Where would McBride go with it? Where would the jury go with it? Yes, Kirby had turned the case around, and he sat down confident of victory.

The court sat hushed and still. There was not a sound from the floor, and the seven men sitting in judgement waited out these long seconds tensely, to see what would transpire from this challenge.

Then there was a stir at the back of the room. A chair scraped the floor as it was pushed back, and Carson stood to his feet. Heads turned incredulously as those present fastened their eyes upon him. Standing there in his buckskin garb, frontiersman written in every aspect of his person, Carson at length spoke.

"Colonel, may I ask a question of Mr Kirby with regard to his very clear statement concerning a witness"

"I am sure Mr Kirby wouldn't mind, would you Mr Kirby"?

Kirby, noting the somewhat nondescript appearance of the questioner, and satisfied within himself that his proposal was beyond defeat, was only too ready to oblige. "Certainly sir, what can I help you with"?

"Well sir, would one credible witness, as you state, be enough to validate the claims these Indians are making, after all it is a strong accusation and it must have taken place a long time ago."

"Certainly, Mr... Mr? "Carson Sir." Yes of course, Carson. Let me repeat. If just one man can be found that is accepted and respected by those gathered here, and who can give credible testimony to what we have just heard concerning Captain Fetterman and a stolen infant, I give my word of honour that I will withdraw my charges without equivocation."

Thank you, sir, I am grateful for this clarification.

With this assurance Carson turned his attention to the Colonel.

Colonel McBride, would I be considered a credible witness were I to give testimony"?

"Carson, please. This is no time to play games, or ask frivolous questions. We are engaged in a very serious court appearance of three men who will hang unless something drastic intervenes. I implore you to not to treat this lightly by these rather distracting questions."

Colonel McBride, I can assure you that my question to you, and the answer I have already received from Mr Kirby, hold the key to this whole issue, but I must have assurance from yourself before I speak.

I therefore ask the question again in all sincerity. Would I be considered by you men to be a respectable and credible witness in this present trial?"

"Well Carson, I do not know where this is leading, but I am going to trust you on it, and I can answer your question if you so desire. You have been a man respected from Fort Laramie to the Bozeman

Trail for decades now, and all our commanders and officers have a high regard for you. Your contribution to the US Army has been exemplary, and without a doubt many lives have been saved through your honest endeavours.

I need hardly elaborate further on what is obvious to all at this table, and I think I can speak for all when I say that yes, you would be to us a very useful, credible and respected witness in this increasingly difficult case, if indeed you can throw light on these proceedings."

"Thank you, sir, please hear me out, and afterwards I will answer any question you may care to ask."

# CHAPTER 21

n 1830 my father and mother arrived here from Plymouth England. My father was a medical doctor, Jason Carson, and he settled west of the Powder River country, perhaps a hundred miles west, in a little township called Twin Forks.

As far as I am aware I was born the following year, and during those early years my parents built up a successful medical practise that is still spoken of today among the older settlers of those parts. For around ten years I often travelled with my father on his many visits to Indian camps, and particularly to the Arapaho. Sometimes the journey was long we would often stay overnight. It was during those years that I struck up a friendship with the chief's son, a young boy called Great Elk. It was returning from one of these camps that my father and mother were killed when their buggy overturned.

I survived, but with injuries so serious that I never made it back to Twin Forks. The Indians who found me took me to an old Methodist couple who were missionaries in those parts and I was reared by them. Because of my injuries I could not remember my first name, and so I have been known ever since as Carson, the name the missionaries found in my father's wallet.

After about ten years with those good people, I struck out on my own, and spent five years in the Sierras trapping and hunting, before coming to the Powder River country, building a cabin and taking a wife. I have been working around these parts for nigh on twenty years now, much of that time scouting for the army.

It was in the fall of '66 that I came on the scene of the massacre spoken of by Great Elk. I must only have been a matter of minutes behind the army patrol, for when I came on the camp it was evident that it was newly happened. Bodies were still warm and blood was still flowing, and the fires had not yet fully taken hold.

I saw the young woman of whom Great Elk speaks, shot through the heart, and I saw the old man slashed to pieces beside a cavalry mount that had been brought down by a lance. I counted 14 women, 8 old men and 16 little children, all butchered, and the dogs and ponies were slain too.

When I came to the Fort a few days later I made enquiries as to that day's patrol from the report in the Forts Incidents Book. I was shown that Mr Fetterman had reported a band of hostiles encountered. The patrol lost one horse and had two troopers slightly injured. All hostiles were killed.

But I knew different Colonel, for I saw the results of his encounter, and not one hostile was among them, unless you count very old men. Thank you, colonel, for your patience.

"Mr Kirby?" The Colonel's voice was loud and clear, and carried a tone of confidence and finality, for Kirby's own statement must now tell against him.

But Mr Kirby was not the honest and honourable man he described himself to be. He had not yet done with this troublesome frontier scout who had so bested him in a matter that to him was black and white. Stolen horses and Indians punished was his credo, and to fail here would be disastrous to his reputation. He had one last card however, and he would play it now. Shook as he was by Carson's testimony, he was determined to besmirch it, but in such a manner as to maintain his own seeming open and honest acceptance.

"Colonel, and colleagues, officers and troopers now in this court. I am sure we are all very impressed with Mr Carson's recollection of what, 16 years ago? It does credit to him. I must confess it is one of the most interesting and intriguing recollections I have ever heard in my frontier service.

Of course we believe it, after all we have given Mr Carson our confidence as to his character as a credible witness.

But while we here today, who know Mr Carson, are happy to accept his testimony, there may be those who will cavil at it on the grounds that it was wholly unproven. If I was a hostile witness to Mr Carson, which of course I am not, I could think of several reasons of how some unfair, unjust and antagonistic people might find argument against it.

Please allow me to illustrate.

Words only gentlemen, that's what the public will say. Nothing substantial or evidential in it. One man's word against another who is no longer here to defend himself. You are all well aware of how rumour and innuendo spreads on the frontier. The camp fires of the West are notorious for big stories, wildly exaggerated recollections and blatant denials of that which decent men are willing to accept from sincere lips. Two things therefore I set before you.

What about this stolen infant. Who ever heard of such? Did any man in this courtroom ever hear of such? An Army Captain stealing an infant, and an Indian infant of all things! Coyotes, wolves perhaps. But for Great Elk to blame Captain Fetterman and his men, just because he saw an iron shod hoof print in the tepee will be considered preposterous.

Also gentlemen, and consider this as outsiders and public at large will almost surely consider it, Mr Carson's alleged association with this Indian as boyhood friends is a stretch indeed.

Has this been known before on the frontier? Is there a shred of evidence that such a friendship ever existed? That his father included the Indian in his medical duties? Can we really believe that his father and mother had travel immunity from the Indians back in those days when so many lost their lives on the trail, and when all travellers needed escorts?

Gentlemen, we are not the public at large, but we know what the public at large will say of this case, and so I speak as I do. We have sometimes unhappy circumstances to deliberate upon. We have done so in this trial, and I think Mr Carson's testimony has brought us to a rather happy conclusion, but the public will be deliberating on this trial for years to come, and both Mr Carson's reputation and that of yourself Colonel, is wide open to the charge of subterfuge and incompetence. His for spinning an unfounded yarn, and yours for allowing it to carry. I for one Colonel do not wish that to happen. Not for you and not for Mr Carson.

If therefore Mr Carson could give us something more tangible than mere words, it would close the mouths of those whose chief aim seems to be criticising our endeavours here on the frontier in very difficult and dangerous circumstances.

Thank you, sirs, for giving attention."

It was a masterstroke of cunning. The Colonel saw the ploy at once, and did not like what he saw. Kirby had put hostile arguments again into the minds of all those present, which was his aim from the start, and he could even now see knowing looks pass between them. They may still feel compelled to free these Indians according to their promise to Carson, but it would now be a hollow victory. Kirby therefore was a winner whichever way it would go, and it showed on his face as he sat down, importantly shuffling some papers as he did so.

"Carson, you have heard the words of Mr Kirby, and sadly it must be said that there are those among the public who may indeed cavil at this court's decision and your testimony. Is there anything further therefore you wish to say on those points raised before we come to a conclusion."

The Colonels words were spoken softly, for he was not deceived by Kirby's profession of sympathy to Carson's reputation, or his own for that matter, and he put the question to Carson in a tone that was devoid of any scepticism or accusation.

"Colonel, I can prove beyond all doubt those two objections are not valid in this case; however they might apply in another."

At this Kirby stopped shuffling his papers and slowly turned his gaze to Carson. He was at once both alert and alarmed. He could hardly believe what Carson had just said, *"prove beyond all doubt"*. What could he mean? What did this ragged scout who continually smelt of buffalo and wood smoke have to say now? For the first time Kirby felt fear in the pit of his stomach. He thought he had won this case; he had been quietly confident in that. But now he began to doubt. He had played his last card. He thought it was an Ace, but Carson's words removed all hope that it was so.

Carson stood at the back of the room and spoke again.

"I was about to ride away that day from the massacre when I heard what I thought at first was a kitten, and upon pulling back the blanket covering the young Indian girl I saw a new born infant. It was immediately obvious to me that this girl had been birthing when she was killed. The child, a girl child, was very cold but still alive, and I picked her up and placed her inside my shirt for warmth. I was on my way to my ranch where my wife was near to give birth herself, and when I arrived I found that she had already done so just two hours previously.

I gave the papoose to her and she immediately put it to her breast as her own. The child lived, she is now 16 years old, and we have reared her as a twin to my own daughter, for there was only a few hours difference in their births. I did not steal the child. I was unaware that a boy had seen the massacre, and that help would soon come, so I did what I thought was necessary to save the child's life. The iron shod hoof print that Great Elk saw in the tepee was from my pony.

I will be happy to allow the Colonel and his wife to speak with my wife and the girl we brought up as our own, and you will find every word I have spoken is true.

As far as my boyhood friendship with great Elk is concerned, I can prove that also. On one of our boyhood adventures Great Elk fell from a tree and broke his right leg just above the ankle. In the same fall he badly gashed his forehead. I ran back to the camp for help and we brought Great Elk home on a pony- drag. My father set the leg and pulled together the remaining skin on his forehead. He used three short buffalo ribs for splints and told the chief he would come back in five days to check on it.

The prisoner here has a bad limp from that injury, and if you remove his headband, I am very sure you will find the evidence of that fall is still there."

The Colonel nodded to Quinncannon and the sergeant walked forward and spoke to Great Elk. All eyes were upon him as the Indian slowly complied with Quinncannon's request.

There it was before them all, a jagged and deep scar that had whitened with age, and seemed to be more pronounced by the copper-coloured skin surrounding it. Kirby looked stunned and slack jawed as he saw his case now demolished.

But Carson was not yet finished. Colonel, I have not seen this man in nigh on 40 years, but I remember a boyhood pact we made back then, and I am hoping Great Elk remembers it too. May I come forward?"

"Certainly Carson." The Colonel, like everyone else in the building, was now spellbound by the unbelievable developments of the last few minutes.

Carson walked the thirty feet or so to where Great Elk was sitting. Till now neither of them had seen the other face to face. Not a sound was heard as the soft tread of Carson's moccasins padded up the floor and stood before the three Indian prisoners. They looked at Carson, and Carson looked at them, his eyes particularly taking in the face and features of Great Elk. Indians age quickly by reason of their outdoor life and the hardships that attend it, but still Carson saw the likeness of the boyhood friend he remembered.

A face recall is chiefly awakened by the set of the eyes, nose and mouth, that small central area that remains identifiable when all else distorts and changes with age, weight or sickness. This was indeed Great Elk, Carson knew it, but would Great Elk remember?

Stretching out his right hand towards him, thumb upwards, Carson saw Great Elk look first at him and then the hand. For a second or two he thought his boyhood friend had forgotten, but then the stony stare of the Plains Indian softened to recognition, then incredulity, and finally the gladness of remembrance.

Standing again slowly, Great Elk stepped forward with outstretched hand, thumb upwards, and spoke in tones of unbelief and wonderment.

"Nathaaan, Nathaaan. Long time Nathaaan, long time. Blood brother, blood brother", and he pressed his thumb against the outstretched thumb of the army scout.

The court, up to now enthralled with the cat and mouse game they perceived had developed between Carson and Kirby, erupted as one man, shouting and gesticulating in support and encouragement of the reunion. The Colonel banged hard on his desk with his pistol butt to restore order, but it was half hearted. He felt elated, but there was a deep anger also at the nearness of a miscarriage of justice, wherein he himself may have sent three innocent men to their deaths.

When order was restored and the Court settled back to its former silence. Kirby jumped to his feet. "Colonel I object"…… "Sit down Kirby, sit down immediately. We have heard enough from you today. We have humoured your ill will against these men for the sake of giving you free rein to exercise your appointed duty of prosecuting counsel. We will hear no more. This case is dismissed forthwith.

Lieutenant Cogburn, allow me to congratulate you on your very thorough defence, and on your spirited and compassionate appeal to reason and decency. Perhaps those who have followed these proceedings may take comfort in the fact that there *can* be justice within the US Army, all we need are men courageous enough to seek it.

Sergeant Quinncannon, take these men to the Sutler's store and see if there is something there they might need. Then go to my quarters and ask my wife to prepare a meal for them. Take Carson with you. A meat wagon was due in today, there may be some items of particular taste to these men, see that they get them. I have work to do, but I will join you all in about an hour.

In the meantime, send the Crow scout to me, the one who led the search party to these men. The army can do without that kind of service.

Court dismissed."

## CHAPTER 22

The meal with the Colonel could have been much more enjoyable had it not been for the fact that Carson had at last found the family his grandmother's letter had hinted at, and having found it, he was impatient to hear the story from the lips of Great Elk.

Around the table he did not wish to elaborate beyond what had been spoken of in the courtroom, and when he had spent what he considered an appropriate time at the table he stood to excuse himself, thanking the Colonel and his wife for their hospitality as he did so.

Once outside Great Elk sent his two companions back to the Sutler's store and he and Carson walked the short distance to the blacksmiths forge and found a quiet corner in which to converse.

To Carson's great surprise he found Great Elk fluent and well versed in English, something which he had hidden even around the table at the meal but now revealed freely to Carson.

As Carson had suspected, he was the grandson of his grand uncle Magus, and like his father Many Horses, had been taught from early childhood this strange new language that the strangers from the East brought with them. Carson let him talk, eager for the story, and Carson seldom interrupted, having asked Great Elk to begin when Magus first appeared on the frontier, and to tell as much as he knew, and ending with the old man's death.

Come first light tomorrow they would set out for the Powder River, where Great Elk would be reunited with his daughter Tappy, Magus's great-granddaughter, but today they would relive the history of their family, so long scattered, but now at last together.


## The Magus story

Magus first appeared in the region long before the white man began to settle, and long before the great trains of their wagons became as many as the wild mustangs that roamed the prairie. Magus had come alone, riding a mule and having two burros laden with those things needed for life in the wilderness. He had followed a tributary of the Snake River northwards till he came to a place far from where any trail led, and, finding a wide bend, had built his cabin against the rock face of an overhanging bluff, sheltered and secluded from the winter blizzards he knew would entomb this land in a shroud of white, and freeze even some lakes to a depth of many feet.

It was as he began to break his own trail northwards that providence smiled on him again, and not for the first time since he left civilisation. He came on an abandoned two wheeled ox cart, of Mexican or Spanish construction, and, apart from being well weathered and of a deep grey colour, still serviceable. The ox that pulled it was still lying between the shafts, or what remained of it. A bleached skull and piece of backbone, the yoke still lying across a neck that no longer felt its weight. As Magus examined his find it became very clear that the previous owner had the same intentions as himself. It was loaded with prospecting accoutrements, and hardware for building a cabin.

Judging by what he saw it was not hard to put together the general picture. The bones between the shafts indicated the beast could go no further, and the owner, no doubt carrying what food supplies he could, had intended to come back for the remainder. After that it was anybody's guess as to why he didn't return. Accident, sickness, killed by Indians? Whatever it was his cart lay now before Magus with vital supplies that would make his life a whole lot easier.

As Magus examined the contents, he could hardly believe his good fortune. Tools, a saw, iron wedges for splitting logs, nails, a chain and a coil of rope that was still usable even though a little weathered. A can of grease and a couple of iron hinges. An iron stove among many other items littered the floor, and pushed into a corner, wedged tightly under side- seat planking, was a small keg of stumping powder[62] and a coil of fuse. There were no food stuffs, nor any sign of any foodstuffs. This no doubt was what the owner had taken with him along with his good intentions when he abandoned the cart.

Magus thought to himself that this had been an ill- advised mission for whoever had undertaken it. Gold fever had distracted the prospector to such a degree that he failed to give attention to what one beast could accomplish, especially over rough and uneven ground, and had paid dearly for his neglect. The luxury of an iron stove was a load in itself, leave aside all the other ironwork, and the cart, too big for one animal, was built of sturdy timbers. The bleached remains between the shafts was ample testimony to the 'get rich quick' attitude prevalent on the frontier, and which had led to countless tragedies.

Before he moved on Magus already had a plan. When he found his spot, he would return with his un-laden beasts and transport what he could first, even if it took a few days. The empty cart could then be hitched to his animals and recovered. He had no need for a cart, but he had great need for the timber it was built of, and pulling it to his cabin would be a lot easier than dismantling it where it lay, and transporting it in pieces.

During his first two years Magus never saw another soul, and no doubt considered himself unseen as well, but it was not so. The Indians of those parts all knew of the stranger, and called him Wolf Man on account of the great beard and long hair that virtually covered his face.

Roving bands would sometimes watch him as he went about his daily chores, and marvelled at the many hours he spent on the great sand bar that lay on the inside of the river bend, digging and washing all day long for the tiny yellow flakes and shining pebbles that had been carried from the mother lode high up in the mountains.

Magus days never changed except when he went hunting or fishing. He was adept at both, and the watching Indians could see that he was never short of meat or fish. His drying racks were always well loaded, and his smoke house could be recognised for miles when the wind was right. The Indians never showed themselves, and left no sign that they had ever been there. Magus had not harmed them, and there was plenty of fish and game for them all. If the Wolf Man wanted to spend his time digging for the yellow metal they would leave him in peace.

Because he had only to construct three walls and a roof, Magus gave attention to building his cabin much longer than the usual. As well as this he had a lean-to on the lee side for firewood, and where his animals could shelter from the worst of the weather.

A stone chimney carried the smoke up the cliff face, from a fireplace that was safe against the ever-present danger of fire, when log walls, becoming dry as tinder, suddenly caught. It was in his cabin that he kept his harnesses and leatherwork, bridles, saddle and tack. All his perishable foodstuffs were likewise protected. Flour, pork, sugar, coffee beans and his supply of salt he had stored with great care, as he did with all items. With the harness hanging on pegs driven into a rock crevice, and utilising local material for seats, shelves and benches, he thought himself very comfortable.

A fall of shale that ran past his cabin provided all he needed for these necessary items of comfort and convenience. These slabs of slate, sometimes three feet long and barely two inches thick were ready made, and light enough for a strong man to handle alone. Placed upon stout wooden pegs, they served admirably, keeping his vittles' dry and safe.

When Magus ran out of necessities he made his way to the nearest township, if such it could be called. Built at the convergence of the trails west to Oregon, east to the great Plains, and south to the Snake River, an enterprising traveller had decided to open a dry-goods store. Out here a man could name his own price for a needed item, and the buyer most often was only too eager to pay it, for it was the only store between there and civilisation. Magus's needs were not many, but coffee, sugar, salt, pork and flour he counted as essentials, and the washings from his sandbar was good currency. Magus was very careful however. He never entered by the same trail into town, nor left the same way.

He entered at darkness and always left before first light, making a detour each time, and, at a suitable vantage point, always and without fail, waited to see if he was being followed. He was deeply troubled at the way in which he had been forced to flee Rannoch, and often pondered on how fickle and fragile life and its circumstances can be. One moment being a respectable member of a community, and in a matter of hours becoming a wanted murderer, and a fugitive from their justice! Since he had received the cobblers warning, he had never trusted another soul, and out here it was no different. What people did not know they could never tell, and that's the way he liked it.

One morning as Magus made his way to his diggings an object caught his eye. Something was caught on a sweeper[63] that lay out over the water, snagged right on the tip where it touched the surface. Light in colour, at first he thought it a dead animal, but as he drew closer, he discerned the prow of a small canoe and the limb of a child hanging over it from the inside. As he ran out into the stream a tiny face then became visible through a tangle of raven locks.

Wading the last few yards Magus freed the canoe from the spur where it had caught and pulled all to the river bank. He then lifted the child from the waterlogged vessel, and found it was a little girl, barely five years old, a mere wisp of humanity. As he carried her quickly to the cabin she uttered a low moan, the only indication that she was still alive.

He knew he had not much time if he was to save her, if indeed she could be saved, but he would do what he could and hope for the best.

Quickly wrapping the child in old woollens, he laid her near the fire. Then, sweeping his breakfast utensils from their slate table, he stood it close against the fire, adding more wood as he did so. As the slate heated he briskly rubbed the child's limbs and body in an effort to generate whatever inner life there was to greater effort, and then laid the now hot stone back on its pegs, before covering it with an old bear skin, fur side up.

Laying the child on a now warm bedding, and still wrapped in the woollens, he covered her with another softer hide, fur side down, from a young elk calf he had worked upon throughout the past winter. Satisfied that he could do no more he then turned to the scalding pot and made ready to make a broth.

Cutting chunks of meat from his latest kill, a young Whitetail, he first filled the pot with these, then he added water till it covered them. He would simmer this for an hour or so and then use from it until the child showed signs of recovery.

When the rich and nourishing mixture was ready Magus salted it, and, cooling some in a cup, began spooning what he could between the child's lips, gently cupping her head forward to allow her to swallow. Slowly but surely his efforts began to pay off, and only when the little girl closed her lips to more did he stop. Magus kept faithful vigil by her side, always ready to offer her the spoon that carried the so needed liquid. He knew it would be touch and go for her. The river flowed mostly from snow melt and glacier higher up, and no one could survive long in it at any time of the year. From this simple fact he knew the little girl's family could not be very far upstream, and he half expected to see a search party combing the river banks for her.

As the child lay hovering between the living and the dead Magus was busy. Taking an old gunnysack, he cut armholes in it, and an opening for her head, using her own tattered garment as a pattern. He finished it off with a drawstring at the waist to bring the garment closer to her body for both warmth and comfort.

He also made her a shawl from his plaid, and a pair of leggings and moccasins from the softer parts of a buffalo hide. They were quite obviously a wilderness production, and he smiled to himself as he viewed the finished articles, but they would keep her warm, of that he was sure, and that was the chief objective in it after all.

All the while Magus worked on these items, the child lay in silence, unmoving, with only the soft and measured rise and fall of her tiny chest as an indication that life was still within her.

For three days and nights she lay like this, while Magus repeatedly heated the stone, then laid her again within the warm folds he had so lovingly prepared for her. Each night, after he had made her comfortable, he knelt beside the barely breathing form and laid hold of God in prayer for her. He did not pray a long prayer, but simply remembered a line or two from a day past and gone, when he had heard another use the words in a similar tragic situation.

*"Dear Lord, preserve this bonnie lass, and make the dread 'death angel' pass*

*Give her life, then may she be, consecrated, all to thee."*

There were a few more lines, but they were said through tears, as his great shoulders heaved in his struggle to intercede for the little one, lying so still and pale before him.

Early on the fourth morning, as he busied himself at the fire, he heard a sound behind him and, turning, he saw the little girl sitting up and staring wildly around her. Catching up the cup and spoon he quickly but gently approached her, hoping that the familiar smell of the liquid might help allay her fears of these strange new surroundings she found herself in. To his immense joy she simply took the cup and drank from it before laying down again, eyes still wide and wondering.

In the weeks and months that followed the child came to accept without question her new home, and as she got stronger, she became inquisitive, and greatly interested in the daily life of her be-whiskered prospector and guardian. Although she rarely uttered a sound, she never strayed far from his side, and would sit for hours watching him dig and then wash his diggings, picking out the shining and attractive flakes and tiny lumps before reaching them to her to put in a jar she carried.

She had begun to do some womanly work about the cabin too. Stirring the flour for the morning pancakes, gathering kindling and attempting the little things that needed attention in cabin life. Slowly Magus came to realise that she had brought him nothing but happiness since she came, and the joy of her daily presence served to highlight for the first time the loneliness he had endured since he fled Rannoch.

One evening, as Magus sat quietly outside the cabin, he suddenly and quite inexplicably turned and looked behind him. Imagine his surprise when he saw the child standing silently just a few feet away. She was smiling broadly, with a delighted smile only a child can accomplish. As Magus rose and turned to greet her, he saw that she had a lapful of blueberries picked from a nearby bramble patch, and she reached him a share from her tiny hand. That little act of affectionate kindness touched him greatly. The openness, innocence and trust she had shown melted his heart. From that day forward he began to realise he loved her as he would his own daughter. Only a foundling, a catch-coat yes, but she was now in his heart, and he did not want to part with her. He was happy in her quiet company, and she in his, and he looked on her as the child he may never have.

It was a relationship that only such a wild and unforgiving wilderness could bring about. A father daughter relationship, but where both parties were poles apart as to their origin. Survival out here was paramount, and so sometimes the most unlikely companions were thrown together from a set of circumstances as diverse as nature itself.

Magus knew in his heart however that it could never be. Even though the child was happy, and she was, this was no place for her. She needed the company and social structures that only a normal family life could give her, and his heart told him he must seek to find her family, or a family willing to have her.

It was true that no one had come downstream looking for her, but that could be for a variety of reasons, and he found no comfort in the thought of his having a right to her on that account.

Perhaps no one saw her fall, and thought she had been killed by a bear or cougar. If she fell into white water[64] perhaps they gave her up for lost there and then. If her disappearance coincided with a tribal dispute or raid, then perhaps they thought of her now as a captive. There were just so many things to prevent a search party coming.

He knew he had only one option, and he had put it off for too long already. Before the Indians left the river from their autumn fishing and curing preparations, he must travel upstream and seek her real family.

Although not speaking her language he knew that she herself would give some indication if and when they came into contact with her tribe or clan. He would sorely miss her presence. Her familiar little figure around his diggings had brought him untold inner joy. But he knew that the longer he put it off the harder it would be to make the decision. Love is a very strong emotion, but when love threatens harm to its object, then it becomes a selfish and harmful force that must be controlled, and Magus knew what he must do in this regard. He loved the child, but he must decide for her good, her long-term prospects.

One morning he began his preparation in earnest. Carrying his belongings to the cabin, he brought inside all that would be the worse for a winter outdoors. He pulled his sluice far above the high-water mark and packed his gold securely in tightly bound leather pokes that he had brought with him for this very purpose. These would travel with him in panniers on the mule, for the burros were prone to spook easily, and he was not about to lose three year's work by being careless.

The child would ride on the mule also, that way he would have his hand on the bridle of all that he held precious in this world. He would walk. He was used to it. The glens and corries of Rannoch were his proving ground, and he had a stride that was perfected on the purpled slopes and mountains of his native land.

He had been preparing for two days now, for there was no room for error when it came to wilderness travel. His list was not a large one. He could not afford space for all he would have liked, but his choices were carefully selected.

A good water skin. Corn dodgers and biscuits. A little jerky and smoked fish. Some fish hooks and line. These lakes contained big trout, one of which could last a man for a week, and they were easily caught. Flour, coffee, salt. Sugar he had run out of. However, a honeycomb, fresh from a hive they found high in an old tree, would be a welcome addition to the biscuit, especially for the child. A small skillet, coffee pot, two cups and two badly chipped plates completed his kitchen needs. His saddlebags carried powder and ball, new flints and tinder, all carefully wrapped.

He had taken the little girl the day before to a small stand of birch where he showed her how to peel back the curling flakes of shedding bark and save them. This was highly combustible, and a handful dropped onto his smouldering tinder would very quickly get a fire going. On the burros he carried an axe, which would double as a hammer in an emergency, a file, a rasp for the animal's hooves, some wire, and the small keg of stumping powder with fuse. A coil of rope completed his preparation.

On his person he had his knife, pistols and long gun, powder- horn and ball, and he was sure that he could shoot enough fresh meat to eke out his supplies. All he needed to pack now was blankets, his saddle roll, and the heavier hides that may be their only source of shelter from rain or early snow. Fire, food and shelter would see them through the worst of weather, and he was confident he had what would suffice.

Before they set out Magus tried to explain to the child what he was doing. To do this he took a piece of dried birch bark and with a charcoal stub drew out a wigwam, a tepee, some boys and girls and a few ponies. It was a simple sketch, childishly simple, but nevertheless conveyed the picture.

Taking the sketch to her he pointed to the dwellings in turn, then to herself. He did this a few times. At first she appeared confused, but when Magus pointed again to the dwellings, and then up river, the child pointed to the tepee and then to herself. Magus was satisfied now that the child remembered her camp well enough to identify a tepee dwelling. He could narrow down the search to tepee dwellers alone, and pass by any camps of wickiups or wigwams.[66]

Pointing north, upstream, and then again at the sketch, Magus made it known they were looking for her tepee. If he thought she would be overjoyed at this he was to be disappointed. She accepted the knowledge without visible emotion, but stared at him intently through it all. Magus knew again that he had made the right decision. The child was already attached to him, and to have delayed longer would have made the coming parting much worse. Prospecting was not for little children. The little one needed family, and company of her own age and tradition.

*** 

The morning dew was heavy upon the ground when they closed the cabin door for the last time and began their journey northwards. There was no trail in these parts. Now and again they would cross a game trail, or follow one for as long as it was travelling in their direction, but for the little party there was nothing to guide them but the river on their left flank. As they made their way through forest and plain in turn, the now warming beams of morning sunlight, shining on the dewy grass before them, sparkled and shone, and gossamer streamers, heavy laden with tiny jewelled droplets, caught their faces as they passed.

The going was reasonably good, the way open and clear, and the river almost always in view. Here and there tall forests reared majestically. Pristine and fresh with the wet of the night still upon them, they were a sight to behold to the eyes of the young prospector, who had spent his last few years on a riverbank, and who now began to see just how much he had missed in doing so.

In the distance, now and again, he could see game, big game. Elk, moose, bear and deer, and marvelled once again at the plentiful abundance of all that was needed to sustain life and comfort.

The child rode easily on the soft pelts covering saddle, looking about her with interest and contentment, and smiling at Magus when sometimes their gaze met.

All the while Magus kept his purpose in view, and his eyes continually scanned the countryside and riverbank for sign of activity. The child's family band need not have been a large one, and he did not want to pass a camp hidden from view by a stand of trees, or otherwise secluded from sight.

Where he could he kept close to the river, for by doing so he could readily see signs of fishing activity, and drying racks and smoke houses would be clearly visible. As the smoke from any fires would be a giveaway, Magus kept mind of this constantly, for the wind did not deceive, even when sight failed. As they climbed higher it became colder, and the nights no longer pleasant and restful.

For three days the pair travelled without seeing a soul, and just as they were about to pitch camp on the third day, he smelt it. The unmistakable and familiar smell of wood smoke. There is nothing so certain to a woodsman or trapper than the smell of a camp fire, and only those familiar with all its comforting associations would recognise it instantly. It was only a fleeting and passing breath, but in the nostrils, it was enough, and he was certain he had caught it. The light was fading, and rather than approach any camp in the darkness Magus decided to wait till morning before he showed himself. His errand may be tricky enough in broad daylight, and he wanted to present his case in the best way possible. First taking careful note of the wind direction, he turned to the necessary chores of making a trail camp.

As he made a fire the little girl busied herself with laying out the supper necessities. A liver and heart from a young mountain ram, fried in its own fat and with a succulence all its own. The skinned-out carcass, wrapped in a piece of canvas, would hold for a day until spit roasted, then it would hold for a few more days. By these means the wilderness provided, and the settler or traveller would never be lacking in sustenance.

As the meat was cooking Magus bent over some second growth saplings and tied them down, first stripping off any small shoots or branches. He then covered these with the hides he brought and placed his bedrolls inside. Whatever the weather these would keep them warm and dry. All through supper a few large stones had been laid against the coals, and when ready Magus took them and laid them out on the ground under the shelter. Then he covered the stones with soft green brush and undergrowth. He then took a double folded blanket and a remaining hide and covered this, thus allowing for a little body to have the soft and warming comfort of uninterrupted sleep.

As dawn broke, and after a cold breakfast, they began the last approach to the camp he knew was there, but was not yet in sight. When they had passed the last of the gentle hills that until now had hidden their goal, they came on a scene that brought him to a standstill in awe and wonder. The first thing he saw was a great lake, and he at once knew he had found the source of his tributary. Beyond that, stretching as far as the eye could see, was a valley of such proportions as to be breath taking, even to the mind of a common man such as Magus was.

It was as if the creating hand of the Almighty had just scooped it out and left the evidence of the same. A wide swathe of green sward, its sides sweeping steeply upwards, was the open gateway to this secluded and majestic scene, and was so like the Coe Glen back home that for the first time since he fled, Magus felt homesick. He had little time however to marvel at the view, for the Indian camp was awake and here and there people were already dismantling the tepees and drying racks.

He was within half a mile of them when they first saw him, and as the word spread the tribe began to gather and stand silently watching this stranger and rider approach. Magus walked purposefully, now and then casting his eyes on the child to see if there was any sign of recognition. The child was young, and two or three months can be a long absence, but she too had fixed her gaze on the scene before her.

Magus walked to within 20 yards of the now sizable company and stood. They seemed transfixed, wondering, perplexed, and Magus began to think he had made a grave mistake in coming here. Then a thought struck him. Turning suddenly, he unfastened the large and brightly coloured brooch that held the plaid shawl round the child's shoulders, and lifted her from off the saddle. Perhaps if they saw her as she used to be they might begin to understand that she was alive and well, and not some ghost or apparition from the dead.

As the little girl stood now before the crowd, dressed only in her little gunny sack smock and moccasins, a low murmur rippled through the gathered number, then a piercing, screaming wail rent the morning air and a young woman dashed forward and embraced the little one, crying all the while and stroking continually the long black braids that Magus had so painstakingly woven and tied off with a little piece of his red plaid lining.

After that it was feasting and dancing, while the details of the lost child were told and retold with the help of a Piute half-breed who had a pretty good grasp of English.

She had been out late one evening on the lake with her father, a young chief called Stone Calf, laying some traps and lines. As he tried to untangle a line he lost his paddle, and swam out to retrieve it. However, the current of the lake outlet had caught it, and as the young chief tried to grab it, the current caught him too. Those watching from the shore could do nothing but watch helplessly as he was swept into the outflow before being lost to view in the surging white water below. But worse was to come. Even as they watched, a tragedy unfolded that would remain imprinted on their minds, and strike them dumb with shock and horror. The canoe carrying the child slowly began to turn and swirl as the undertow caught it also. The child's screams were of no avail, serving only to worsen the unfolding scene. Suddenly it too was beyond help, and finally disappeared into the deep ravine to be lost to sight and all hope.

No one came downriver to search for them, because the river had never given up its dead before, and this time would be no different. That was why the Indians called it, *The River of No Return*. The shock therefore of seeing the child again had held them in unbelief, until Magus set the child on the ground before them.

As Magus lay down that night to sleep, he allowed his mind to cover the whole story once again. He had reckoned he had walked about 60 miles. At the rate of river flow he judged that the canoe had been on the water 12 hours or more, and had only survived the rapids because of its birch bark construction. Unladen, except for a little child, it had floated like an autumn leaf, its own fragility becoming its safety. Magus had never openly spoken of the details of the child's deliverance, but he was already convinced in his own mind that it was a miracle. Although far from home, he had not forgotten the Bible lessons taught him at his mother's knee, and he was still a firm believer in the providence of a loving God. He was thankful for the child's safety, glad she had come to him, and he knew he had done the right thing by bringing her home. A few days later however the full implications of his care and concern became known to him.

One morning, as he left his makeshift camp, he saw around six Indians seated in a semi-circle twenty yards away, and inside the circle was the little girl and her mother, seated on a hide and with their belongings lying beside them.

The men greeted Magus in their usual friendly way and called to him to join them. As he neared the group the little one, Nu-tsi-pa,[67] ran to him and caught him by the hand, walking the last few yards with him.

As Magus approached, they bade him sit down with them, and their leader, the chief who succeeded Stone Calf, became their spokesman. Speaking through the Paiute half-breed, what he had to say astounded Magus.

The whole tribe held Magus in great praise and admiration. So much so that he had taken on the role of 'Wise Man' within the tribe, and he was now 'Big Medicine'. What he had done could only be matched by a similar sacrificial gift from them to him. They had heard many good words from white men before, but they had never yet seen good acts without words.

To have delivered the only daughter of Stone Calf back to the tribe as Magus had done, was an honour beyond words to express, and they had now come to meet that honour, and allow him to see that the Shoshone people were a people that do not forget their true friends.

As Magus listened to all this, and saw how sincerely the words were spoken, with the others nodding assent every now and then, he began to feel a little apprehensive as to what these people had in mind. He had no thought of himself as being 'Big Medicine'. He did not want to be 'Big Medicine' He was not a man who desired recognition, and he feared that through all this his secret may be made known, and his fleeing to the frontier might now be a lost venture. Although Magus had received the news of the gamekeeper's confession, and that he was now free to return to Rannoch, he did not trust the news, and such was the passage of time spent alone here, he had lost the desire to return, and was happy to live far from the people who would have hanged him. He sat therefore with bated breath as he waited for the young man to finish.

Finally, the chief stood, and taking the mother and child by the hand, presented them to Magus with the words, "Stone Calf's woman and Stone Calf's child, you alone out of all our tribe have earned the right to have them."

Magus boasted throughout his life that his marriage was like that of Isaac and Rebecca. Short on trappings but long on blessings.

Thus it was that Carson's Grand uncle Magus became accepted within the Indian Nation, and as he remained with them his reputation grew year by year, until he achieved a place and position never before accomplished among them. He died an old man and full of days, and in his last days the little girl he had pulled from the river tended him like a daughter.

He had only one request to make concerning his funeral, that it would be a Christian burial, and that portions of his Bible, marked out and designated by him, be read out and translated to the hearers. It had been his lifelong desire to see his adopted people come to the truth of Redemption's story. The Sacrificial death of Christ, and the hope and certainty of the resurrection to all those who accepted him as their Lord in this life.

The Indians were well aware of the faith Magus had; a faith so different from their own. He and his family had lived by it daily for decades among them, and lived well too, bright examples to them all. It never occurred to them therefore to question his last request. To the very end they had respected and revered him, and many secretly felt that the spirit and influence of the great man was still among them. Guiding them, protecting them, praying for them!

***

There would be much more to this story in the coming days Carson thought, but the blacksmith had long gone and the forge was in darkness. Over in a corner the dull red glow of the firepan was still visible, but only just. The ever-darkening crust of cooling cinder would soon smother it too, and the two men would call it a night. They had talked for hours, but what a story. Carson was deeply moved at the revelations, and proud too. His Grand uncle was a frontiersman, self-taught and successful, and had left behind kin of which he could be proud also.

One day soon he would tell Great Elk the Rannoch side of his grandfather's history, and of the accident that claimed his own father and mother. He would also tell him of his own journey up till now. His upbringing by the missionaries, and the Christian influence still upon his life to this very day, guiding him even as he scouted, and as he sought to protect his people from the many cruelties of the army.

Yes, he would tell him, and Magus, Prairie Flower and Ta-pun-sa-win would make it much easier for him, for he would be speaking to Great Elk as one of his own, and not as a white intruder!

# CHAPTER 23

The child squealed with delight as the pony moved forward, tiny hands holding tiny fistfuls of hair that hung in silken waves from its neck. Nathan Carson moved too, for he had a handful of the shirt that hung loosely around the boy, and as he walked alongside his joy was complete.

Little Abe was his first grandchild. The boy that had accompanied his father to Carson's spread so many years ago, motherless, heartbroken and penniless, had come to years. Honest as the morning light, innocent as an unbroken colt, straight and strong as the lodge pole pines that grew down by the river, Abe Anderson was all that Carson could wish in a son-in-law. His father Jacob never married again, preferring to have the memories of his childhood sweetheart, and throwing himself into the endless chores that needed daily attention on a horse ranch.

It was indeed a fortuitous arrangement for Carson, and when he thought of the day he first spoke to Jacob and young Abe, he also thought of the promise Grandma Turner had instilled into him from the Book of Ecclesiastes.

*"Cast thy bread upon the waters, for thou shall find it after many days".*

His daughter Helen had found happiness in the cabin Abe had built for her. She was frontier through and through, and was neither dazzled nor distracted by Eastern ways, fashions or grandeur.

Carson loved her, and thanked the good Lord every day for her. Now she had borne him a grandchild, and he was content.

Prairie Flower was at the pony's head, coaxing it gently forward, her once raven locks now streaked with grey. Carson thought her more beautiful now than ever, for the grey hairs represented to him the long years of toil she so willingly gave, that she might prove a worthy wife.

Enduring his long absences, toiling and labouring in the fields to replenish the root cellar against the time of winter storms, and to provide for all the pressing daily household needs bringing up a family entail. Carson loved her dearly.

In the beginning he thought he loved her, but he realised now that true love was more than his hearts emotions back then. At first he had liked her. Oh, he had liked her a lot, but as the years rolled on he grew to love her, for Carson found that real love is a gradual, ever-growing bond that far surpasses any youthful emotion. His early liking had matured and grown, and it was now in the full flower, as opposed to the bud of his early attraction. He had filed a claim on two more sections, and he had now enough land for them all, including grandchildren. Good grazing, good water and good timber. He needed nothing more.

As he viewed her now against the background of the Montana sunset, and the rolling hills and mountains of his own range, he could not have been happier. He had finally done with the army. He had struggled with his conscience long enough. After the court case he was disgusted, and yet felt so powerless to do anything about it. It was when word began to spread of a new scheme begun the year before however that brought him to his final decision.

Lieutenant Richard Pratt[68] had founded an institution whereby Indian children were kidnapped, taken forcibly from their reservations, and placed in specially designed boarding schools where they were to undergo a 'civilisation' programme.

Within these walls all sorts of abuse were reported. Cruel punishment was the lot of any who did not obey to the letter the harsh and cruel regime.

Sickness was rife and death was a common visitor. Children's hair was cut and they were forbidden to speak their mother tongue. Those who were caught doing so were made to eat soap to cleanse their mouth from the evil of such.

It was altogether too much for Carson. One morning he simply saddled his horse and rode out of the Fort without looking back. He left a note for the commanding officer, thanking him for his service to him, and for his support when needed. It was a decision he never regretted. He could not influence the men in power that cooked up these crazy ideas, but he could distance himself from them, and show his disapproval by doing so.

In the gathering twilight they heard the voice of Ma Harte calling. It was suppertime, and Ma Harte, a neighbour, had come to help with the cooking. Grandma Turner, by reason of age and 'rhumatiz' she said, had taken on strictly supervisory roles! Tonight would be special. It was little Abe's 3rd birthday, and visitors were expected. Even now Carson could see them coming. He had spotted their dust an hour ago and now they had arrived.

Silhouetted against the crimson of the suns last remaining light, the party were a welcome sight, for Carson could identify the figure of Tap-un-sa-win, Tappy, who had brought them so much happiness since the day he had laid her in Prairie Flowers arms. She rode close to her husband on one of Carson's best mounts, his gift to her on wedding day. He felt blest indeed that his girls, daughters both in his heart, had married well and were happy. What more could a father want than this?

As the group of mounted visitors drew nearer Carson's eyes went to Great Elk. Dressed in his eagle feather headdress, new buckskins beaded and fringed, he looked a fine figure indeed. Proud, unbowed, dignified. The gift of his long-lost daughter had put new life into him, and Carson had in him a trusted companion. Although Great Elk had settled on the Tongue River Reservation, he and Carson had renewed their childhood bond, and often met to talk over old times and lament present times!

Tonight however there would be none of that. A Whitetail deer had been on the coals all day, the Harte boys taking turns at the spit, while Ma Harte had skillets just brimming with savouries, and there were fruits aplenty to finish off, for Jacob Anderson had planted the seedlings his wife had brought for California, and his orchard was the talk for miles around.

When the court dismissed that day the Colonel and his wife became host to a strange mixture of 1880s frontier life. Quinncannon, Sergeant, US Cavalry, Irish through and through. Carson, frontier scout and guide. The three Indians, Arapaho, and the Colonel, English born and West Point taught.

Carson and Great Elk often reminisced of those days. They laughed when they spoke of Kirby, for he immediately requested a transfer and took his overdue leave till his application was granted. They sobered however when they spoke of how close they had come to tragedy.

Two days after the court case buffalo hunters brought the stolen horses to the Fort. They recognised them from the harness that still hung from them, and scared off the young Indians who were leading them. Finding the horses was an opportunity too good for the hunters to pass up, for they knew the army would repay them well in ammunition, which was always welcome, and which was a well-known practice here on the Plains.

The Indian reservations were a source of grief to the two old friends, as was the near extinction of the buffalo herds. When the hunters were at work the Plains stank with the decaying carcasses, while the Indians looked on helplessly at a practice that was beyond their minds to grasp.

Carson had desired Great Elk to come and live on his ranch in the Powder River country, but he refused to leave his people to reservation life while he himself would be free. It was a noble and loyal choice, and served to give Carson an even greater appreciation of the Indian character.

Tap-un-sa-win had married a neighbouring settler's boy, and had remained on the ranch, but she visited her father and her people twice a year and saw to it that they were not in hardship. This would be her last trip for a little while however, for Great Elk and Carson would soon be sharing the role of grandfather!

The Whitetail on the spit had become considerably smaller, and the visitors had moved outdoors to find a little room, for the cabin was not built with such a large gathering in mind. A fire had been lit near the barn and the people gravitated towards it, pumpkin pie balanced on hands that were already overloaded with other viands. Someone produced a fiddle and the music began. The older folks hung back a little, but the bolder of the youth broke the ice, and soon the dust was rising to the fiddle's squeaking and squealing.

It was socialising at its best and most innocent. Neighbourliness open and sincere. It was how people of the frontier got to know one another. It was how young people found their life's partner in a land that was still in the making, and that one day, in the fullness of time, Carson hoped would become a great nation. A land where all men could find acceptance on equal terms, and freedom to express their innermost hopes and concerns without fear of persecution or violence. He would not be alive to see this, but he fervently hoped that it would come. That after the carnage he had witnessed in his short lifetime, the scriptures would surely come to pass, when *"swords would at last be made into plough shares, and spears into pruning hooks, and that nations would not learn war any more"*.

Carson and Prairie Flower stood in the shadow of the barn, the firelight's flickering glow catching the tenderness that was evident between them. He put an arm round her waist and pulled her closer to him.

There was so much he had wanted to say at this moment, but he found himself lost for words. He had already said it to the hills, and it was good. He said it to the stars and it was better, and when he said it to the moon it was perfect. But now, with his beloved Prairie Flower in his embrace, he found he could not speak. His heart was too full for words.

**THE END**

# Our Story

## Roots

I was born on August 6, 1947, into the austerity of post-war Northern Ireland. Food rationing was still with us, so much so that I never remember our weekly shopping called anything more than 'The rations.' Never shopping, never groceries, but 'The rations.'

I came from a poor working-class family and background. When my dad was demobbed in 1946, he returned with very little to show for his service or war wound. Our first home, in the severest winter in living memory to that time, was a single room corrugated iron shed, a former country confectionary shop, 20 x 10 feet, at that time utilised as rented accommodation. We would make fourteen house moves from my birth, and I remember all but two of them. I was 11 years old before we got a house with running water, electricity, and an outside flush toilet!

Although my dad was always a hard worker, in the 50s' unemployment was often a problem, and those were hard times for us as I remember. Even though money was not plentiful in my early life, I was never hungry at home, but I was often hungry at school. Any lunch I carried to school was eaten by mid-morning if not before, and it was a long day thereafter.

## Education

However, as every cloud has a silver lining, mine had one too! Perhaps because of our very limited recreational opportunities, we had only a radio to keep us abreast of events in the outside world, I turned to reading at every opportunity. I would have read anything, and often did so. Reading material was extremely difficult to find, and soap wrappings, or packaging, or the instructions on the tins of baby milk powder very often took my attention in the absence of something more edifying! Always and in every place, I would read whatever presented itself. Road signs. Warning signs, or directional signs, even though I was near to home and knew exactly where I was! We never had the luxury of a weekly children's comic or magazine, not even a daily newspaper, so my reading possibilities were slim indeed.

As my schooling progressed, and I was introduced to children's reading books, my reading needs were finally met, and although it took me a while to find my feet as it were, our class reading became my most interesting school subject. We used the Wide Range Reader series, wherein were very interesting stories. Some historical, some fiction, but all exciting. Years later in High school, we had a young new English teacher, and she introduced us to poetry, namely, 'Poems of Spirit and Action.' Her classes were no weary drudgery as others often were, for she made those bygone characters come alive. My imagination was further captivated, and these poems brought images to my mind of the exploits of yesteryear, of men who made history by their courage, boldness, and daring.

Reading became my chief interest, and, even at home, an escape to a private world where I could find challenge, excitement and pleasure. I thank God for this gift, for it is a gift, a gift that has stood me in good stead right throughout my life, and still continues to do so. But I have digressed.

There was never any attempt in our home to excel academically. We went to school as a legal requirement, and that was that. In later life it remains as one of my greatest regrets that I missed a proper education. I am not blaming my parents for this. Not at all. That was the way we were. Paradoxically, I must confess that as a parent myself I did not have a great zeal for our six children's further education. That they did well in life is more praise to them and their mum than it's to me.

I never liked sports, either at school or in later life, nor did I participate in them, except it were compulsory. Neither competition or ambition ever attracted me, and I often wonder why people are so given to these things which, in so many instances, involves detriment, jealousies or hurt to others.

**Teenage Years**

From a very early age however, a paternal family tradition was strong in me, and fishing, hunting and shooting have remained with me throughout my life. From small game shooting with a shotgun to large game with a full-bore rifle, and the dressing and butchering of the same, I have always maintained an interest and derived great satisfaction.

Even now, the smell of a campfire's wood smoke ever evokes the nostalgia of outdoor living. Of running a long line for pike on some secluded lake, or savouring tasty trout, encased whole in clay and cooked on hot embers. Even today road kills are not ignored, and if I cannot use them, I will always know someone who can!

By the time I left school in 1962 things had improved employment-wise in Northern Ireland and I found plenty of work, much of it with my dad in construction and roadworks etc. In those years Dad taught me pretty much all I know, and his work ethos was infectious. I think it one of the greatest DNA legacies I could ever wish to have.

Sadly, my later teens brought their challenges, and what with other issues, resulted in much domestic upheaval. The failure of a first attempt at leaving home did not deter me on a second occasion, and I spent the winter of '67-68 working for Hackney Borough Council, London. Home again, and marrying in September 1968, my life had all the appearance of a continuation of my previous twenty-odd years, and nothing is glorifying in relating the details of sin and shame. Suffice it to say the intervening Grace of God found me and delivered me, and from that point onwards my life took on a whole new meaning.

## A New Beginning

On April 12, 1970, when I was 23 years old, from living a dissolute life and far from the kingdom, I was brought to a crisis point with a great inner conviction of my sinful and evil ways, and a dread of the judgement of the Almighty. It was in the quietness of a fireside conversation that I was finally led to see, from the Scriptures, that Christ was willing to save me if I was truly penitent, and accepted by faith alone his promise of salvation.

When the light and understanding of His Words finally dawned upon my soul, I there and then got on my knees, confessed my sinful condition, and accepted His blessed offer as contained in John's Gospel chapter 6:37, *"All that the father giveth me shall come to me; and him that cometh to me I will in no wise cast out."*

My wife Irene trusted Christ the same evening. It was indeed a double miracle for this young couple.

From that very instant I knew I was saved to serve. Strange as it is to relate, and perhaps strange that I should say so, but I knew there and then that this could be no 'Sunday only' experience. I realised immediately I had done something and entered into something that was life-changing. It could be no other way as I understood it.

How all this would happen I did not know, for I had no education worth speaking of, and what form it would take I did not know, for I was untaught in the Scriptures of truth, but I knew it must happen, for mortals do not meet with the Lord of Glory and come away unchanged!

From that fireside conversion, this salvation would now become the sole purpose and activity of my life and being. To this end I went back to school (night classes) and achieved basic but necessary grades in preparation for what I felt was the leading of the Lord for my life.

## The Kindness of Strangers

It was after completing my 'schooling,' that my wife and I took a major step of faith, by placing ourselves, our family and our future entirely into the Lord's hands. It came about like this.

I had a very good position in a precast concrete works, and I got on very well with my employers and workmates, who were Roman Catholics, even though for long periods over the years I was the only Protestant among them. It is not too much to say that when I finally left that employment, I missed it greatly, and still look back on that period of my life as the happiest of all.

But to come back to the story.

I gave notice one day to my employer that I was leaving.

Upon asking me why I was leaving I was honest with them and explained that I felt led to enter the Christian ministry, and in preparation for that I was going to Bible school, which required two days of attendance each week, plus home study material, and I could not in fairness ask them for such an arrangement. To their great credit, and to my greater gratitude, they would have none of it. I was told to come and do whatever hours I could, keep a note of them and present them for payment.

After two years of this arrangement, I was placed as a student in a little church 100 miles away, and my employers duly arrived at our door with a lorry and transported us, lock, stock and barrel to our new home at absolutely no cost whatever. I will never forget them for their kindness.

The successful conclusion of the four-year course in theology, which commenced in 1974, led me to minister in two churches over the next 20 years.

## Broader Horizons

After a 15-year pulpit service in my second charge, I resigned in September 1996 to pioneer an evangelical mission in a semi-arid region of Eastern Kenya. Since a visit to missionaries in 1990, the plight of Africa's multitudes stirred my heart to overflowing. Indeed, it was during that very visit that I was led once again to make another decision that would be life-changing.

Initially it was a personal burden, but needless to say such a venture could not long remain personal. On leaving the pulpit ministry, it was made apparent to me that the missionary work I envisaged was more than the confines or mission strategy my denomination would allow, and my plans and work became independent. The transition to independence was not without its difficulties, and the mission was not born without the birth pangs commonly experienced by new ventures. But born it was, even though this Founder had gone well beyond the usual pioneering stage in life.

I was nearing 50-years of age, dependent on my Church for accommodation, and my retirement plans, such as they were, tied up in our Church Pension Scheme. We had no savings, no property, and no 'safety net' should my venture fail, and to take this step of faith would mean abandoning everything.

But I had the call of God in my heart, and again He provided in a most remarkable way. The congregation I ministered in sponsored me for one year, till I had the opportunity to establish the mission, and allowed us to remain in their Church house until we could purchase our own. It was indeed a generous and appreciated support, and has not been forgotten by us.

## In the House of My Friends

From the very outset, this new work that I commenced suffered great opposition, especially from the leaders of my denomination, and from the Missionary in Africa, even though I would be 400 miles from their endeavours!

My ministerial colleagues however threw their weight behind it, by giving me opportunity to present it to their congregations. By that means the mission grew in quite a remarkable way. What a success it became in the hearts and minds of our people in Northern Ireland.

From literally counting small change from collecting boxes on our kitchen table in 1996, in 22 years the annual income had grown to over quarter of a million pounds by May 2018. In the intervening years, with the understanding, support and help of my wife Irene, we went ahead with our plans and, under God, lived to see the vision He had given us come to pass.


## Evangelism Through Humanitarian Means

Ours was not a social gospel, although it was often maligned as such. We simply brought to the fore that oft neglected truth, that there is a very real social side to the true gospel! A brief overview may be helpful to enable the reader to understand our fieldwork in this regard. We built a medical clinic as our base, and from there we extended over the years as opportunity allowed. Outreach medical clinics, two orphanages, evangelistic outreach programmes, evangelical churches and several schools built, a Bible school for pastors and students, a tailoring and sewing class for young girls who perhaps had never gone to school, and assisting the wider community where we could, especially in food for work schemes and providing water wells. Gospel literature was distributed widely and Bibles were bought for Secondary school pupils.

We fed the hungry in times of famine and counted it a privilege to do so. This became our life's joy. When I look back now to our time there, it is images of these things that fill our minds and hearts. It was indeed a thriving, growing work, and every year we had an annual report for our home supporters whereby we showed, by film, what we had achieved.

It was my great inner satisfaction that the Word of life was being preached to thousands, and our various other ministries to them, all accomplished in Jesus' name, touched the lives of as many more. As Sowers of the good seed we were grateful for those listening ears, and we trusted the Lord to give them understanding hearts.

## The Danger of Presumption

I would like to give a glowing report of many souls getting saved during our years there, but I cannot. Of course there were those who professed Christ, and there were a few who evidenced the ongoing fruit of true repentance, but I cannot say more than this.

*"Salvation is of the Lord."* Jonah 2:9. No human intellect or intelligence can lay claim to assisting, originating, or recognising with certainty this Divine miracle of salvation in the souls of His chosen. I view with great scepticism the very positive yet shallow claims some are prepared to make of 'souls saved' on the foreign field. These professions of faith, sometimes made after the excitement of a charismatic performance by a visiting preacher, or the sketchiest witnessing on a home visit deep in the bush, and through an interpreter, must not be taken and counted as 'proof' of the work of the Lord.

The mature evangelist, taught in the Scriptures, will know from experience how great is the number who fall away after a profession of faith, even in a civilised, progressive society, let alone among those to who can neither read or write, and perhaps hearing a message they never heard before! He will also know from the book of Acts alone just how difficult it is to see men and women brought to a true knowledge of salvation, and just how focused those early sermons of the apostles were on expounding the Scriptures. Christ's Deity, His plan of redemption. The Blood atonement. The Resurrection of Christ. Repentance from sin, and the Resurrection of the dead. Eternity alone therefore will reveal the fruit of our years there, and we sincerely pray that it will be much fruit. Beyond that, I cannot claim more.

Very early on in 1996, when natural concerns came to mind about what we should do concerning a home for ourselves, the Lord gave me a very definite word of counsel. It was from the Book of Proverbs 24:27. *"Prepare thy work without, and make it fit for thyself in the field; and afterwards build thine house."*

What a word it was to me back then, and how faithful the Lord proved to be in our obedience to it. And what a word it is to all who may be in the valley of decision. *First things first* God says, and if the *first* things are *His* things, then all else will fall into place. They did so with my going Independent. They did so with my employment. They did so by leaving my pulpit charge, and they did so on the mission field. It grew far beyond anything our denomination had ever seen before or since, and demonstrated to all who had so ungraciously and bitterly opposed it, that oft forgotten truth, '*when the Lord opens a door, no man can shut it*'.

It was in May 2018, with the mission at its apex, that I resigned. Allowing others, evidently eager to take the reins of this eminently successful mission, to have their opportunity.

My wife and I were 22-years in the Kenyan project.

# APPENDIX

[1]**Fetterman:** His arrogance and disrespect towards the Indian is well documented. I have used his name as a literary device only in the atrocity where the papoose was found, but his own subsequent action, wherein he led his entire command to their deaths, may be taken as a sample of his selfish recklessness, and a fatal ignorance of Indian fighting.

[2]**Pemmican:** Traditionally, a mixture of dried meat from buffalo, moose or elk, any meat in fact, pounded small, and mixed with dried nuts, berries, or fruits. Rendered fat, buffalo or bear fat, was then poured over and it was stirred well to encase thoroughly all the dry ingredients. This mix was highly nutritious, contained all the nourishment needed for good health, and was an important addition for a tribe or family's winter needs. It kept edible for a long time, and the destruction of this winter staple in a punitive raid was a hard blow to an already hungry and starving people.

[3]**Parfletche:** Leather or hide bag, basket or satchel used for storing or carrying foodstuffs or other items.

[4]**Pelts:** Animal skins.

[5]The seventh President of the United States from 1829 to 1837.

[6]**Stoop:** Raised walkway that fronted many cabins, and was sheltered by the overhang from the roof.

[7]**Pony drag:** A Travois. A stretcher slung between two poles, pulled by a pony or horse.

[8]**Rosebud Creek:** Is a tributary to the Yellowstone River in Bighorn County, Montana.

[9]**Treed:** Said of an Opossum, or Raccoon, chased by hounds, when it runs up a tree for safety.

[10]**Cornpone:** Maize meal mixed with water, salt, and oil or hog fat. Heavier than cornbread which usually contains eggs, butter, milk, flour and baking powder.

[11]**Chitlins:** Animal intestines emptied of their contents and washed. They can be cooked different ways, but cutting small and roasting is a popular method.

[12]**Nigger:** Until 1960, when it became independent, Niger was a West African French colony to the north of present-day Nigeria. Both countries took their name from the river Niger which flowed through them. The word Niger carried the French pronunciation, and was therefore 'Neeger.' While the Latin word for the colour black is also Niger, it is a matter of some dispute that it was from this Latin word that 'Nigger' became synonymous with those of the Black race. The more probable explanation however is not hard to find.

Although the English and American pronunciation of this word today is Nai-juh, with a soft G, to the early colonisers and pioneers of a past age, etymology and exactitude in things linguistic was hardly a priority. What is clear however is that the word Niger was a perfectly natural, reasonable and indeed inevitable title for people who came from West Africa, and the fact that we still use generic terms today for race description is beyond dispute.

As we still speak today of the Irish, the Scots, the Welsh etc, it is not difficult to accept that those of a past age did the same, and would have spoken similiarly of the Nigers, or 'Neegers', i.e. those from Africa. Thus when old Zack addressed young Carson, he meant no disrespect whatsoever. "....you ain't never seen a 'Neeger' before....?"

Not all who used the word therefore did so in a pejorative manner, but because of the cruelty and wickedness imposed, (and allowed) upon these unfortunates, the term degenerated to a racial slur, and became a descriptive term for what was widely considered then as a 'less than human' being, literally so. This word has since been demonised, and become a point of controversy even to the present day.

Regretfully, although the Slave trade of past centuries may be considered as the greatest single atrocity civilisation has ever inflicted on fellow human beings, and is abhorred today by every right-thinking person, the passage of time has not laid to rest the events of that tragic period for many in the present day.

I see a trend that runs through various ethnic strands of the Black community. From MPs, celebrities, actors, TV personalities, athletes, and Black activists, there is hostility, an edge, a 'chip on the shoulder' attitude, a very evident pushing of the Black issue, and a 'too ready' mind - set to raise again the evils of Slavery as a stick to beat the White race with. Seeking apologies from this generation for the past sins of another, some reverting to serious public disorder to make their point known!

Such behaviour and activity is hardly in the interests of progressive, forward thinking in support of their race, and only provides grist to the mills of White racists, White supremacists, giving them an excuse for their ongoing hatred of all things Black.

We must accept each generation for what they are of themselves, for they cannot be held accountable for the sins of centuries past, and it is beyond ridiculous to expect such. If those of one colour keep reminding those of another colour of the wrongs done to them by their forefathers, is not this in itself racism?

Furthermore, a society that allows or panders to this growing undertone of historic petulance, anger, ridicule, fault finding, nit-picking or such an exaggerated sensitivity that they will not even articulate the word 'nigger', but use instead a childish substitute euphemism, 'The N Word', are merely encouraging their own nemesis. Does not history teach us that appeasement is never enough!

As someone who has spent 30 odd years in service to the Black race, I have an ongoing concern for what I see still of injustice and oppression concerning them. I see Africa, 'an open sore on the face of humanity.' The suffering Lazarus lying at the rich man's gate. To all Black/coloured critics therefore of Britain's dark past in this regard, I say this.

Bitterness, anger, ridicule, nit-picking, historic apologies etc, never put a bowl of porridge before a hungry infant. Never sponsored a poor child through school. Never mended a broken heart. Never provided a well of clean water. Never provided a thatch for a widow's roof. Never won trust, loyalty or affection for a cause. There is a better way, a more productive way to show ethnic loyalty. Is not compassion for the living of the present age a more enduring legacy than division and strife for the dead of an age that is gone?

[13]**Burros:** Small donkeys, used for carrying loads. Mules and donkeys could adapt more easily to harsh conditions of weather or diet, and were more valuable for travel on that account.

[14]**Flintlock:** A system of ignition for early firearms. A French invention of the early 17th Century, 1610. In various forms it served its purpose well for 200 years. It was not until 1810 or thereabouts that Rev Alexander Forsyth, of Belhelvie, Aberdeenshire, invented an ignition system contained in one small cap. This Cap was a tiny hollow cylinder, made of metal and closed at one end, and containing a small amount of shock sensitive material, (Fulminate of mercury). This cap was placed on a hollow nipple that led directly to the main powder charge within the breech of a muzzle-loading firearm.

Forsyth's 'percussion' system made the flint and flash pan obsolete, for it allowed the cap, when struck, to send the ignition flame directly to the charge within the breech. More reliable, safer, and more effective too in wet conditions or when hunting game. Forsyth's system was truly a game-changer in the evolution of firearms. Today's modern cartridge is merely an enlarged improvement on Forsyth's invention. For within the modern cartridge we have primer, propellant and projectile in one sealed unit!

[15]**Frizzen:** The L shaped piece of steel hinged at the breech of a Flintlock weapon, and struck by the falling hammer. The hammer, having a piece of flint held in place by a set of jaws, carries the flint forward to strike the steel when the trigger is pulled. The resulting sparks ignited a small powder charge in the flashpan below, which in turn, through a small touchhole, ignited the main charge within the breech.

[16]**Pan:** The small cupped receptacle that held the priming powder on the breech of an early firearm. When closed the Frizzen covered it, but the falling hammer and flint threw back the frizzen while provided the spark for ignition. The touchhole that led to the inner breech provided the means of the pan's ignited powder reaching the main charge.

[17]**Flash in the pan:** This happens when the primer alone ignites, and the main charge remains ineffective as a consequence. This has given rise to our well-known term for a promising beginning which fizzles out - A flash in the pan!

[18]**Hang fire:** This occurred when the ignition flame from the pan or cap was delayed in its transmission to the main charge, or the main charge failed to catch immediately. Many a man was killed when he did not wait those vital moments to ascertain if or not a delayed ignition was still in progress! In old flintlock and percussion guns damp was very often the cause, or poor-quality powder or caps. A partly blocked vent

or touch hole would also have contributed to this common danger. In modern weapons 'hang fires' still occur due mainly to faulty primers.

[19]**Buffalo chips:** Essentially cowpats. Sun-dried; they were often the only means of cooking when timber was not to be had on the plains.

[20]**Squashes:** Butternut, Pumpkins or such like fruits, usually used and cooked as vegetables.

[21]**Curly Maple:** Used for knife handles and gunstocks for centuries, no other wood has this unique feature. Compression rings, bands or curls, running perpendicular to the grain, sets this wood apart for beauty and elegance. The feature becomes more noticeable when a finish is applied.

[22]**Patch box:** A small compartment cut into a rifle stock and covered by a hinged lid. It was named after the contents it usually held, the cloth patches for the powder and ball load.

[23]**Trapper cured:** Sun dried or air-dried hides.

[24]**Sear:** Mechanism that holds the bolt, firing pin, or hammer under tension, until the trigger pressure is reached to release it.

[25]**Travel or Creep:** Terms used of a trigger that has a lot of first pressure movement before the actual release is accomplished. A trigger ought to release suddenly, like the snap of a biscuit, without undue and uncertain previous movement.

[26]**Windage:** The effect a prevailing cross wind might have on a bullet, especially at long range, and requiring an allowance by either sight adjustment or by shifting the aiming spot to compensate. A .50 calibre slug could handle windage better than a lighter calibre, therefore reducing the need for adjustment unless wind conditions were so severe as to call for it.

[27]**Holdover:** Aiming a little high above a distant target to compensate for 'bullet drop' at long range.

[28]**Burning off:** The author has eaten this, with chitlins too, on many an occasion, and enjoyed it immensely.

[29]**Donner Party:** A group of immigrants who were stranded in the Sierra Nevada during a blizzard in 1846/47. They were on their way to California, but took a 'short cut' on the advice of an inexperienced and reckless trail guide! Out of 87 souls who set out only 48 survived. The survivors ate the dead, and two Indian guides were killed and eaten. The whole sad story is one of ineptitude and carelessness.

[30]**Cord:** A measurement of chopped firewood, 4 feet x 4 feet X 8 feet.

[31]**Root Cellar:** Usually a subterranean structure, dark and cool. Such was a must for the pioneer settler for providing conditions whereby fruit, vegetables and salted meat could be kept edible for months without refrigeration.

[32]**Heart shot:** A common occurrence with large animals. The heart can be literally shredded and yet the beast may run a short distance. The author has witnessed this phenomenon for himself.

[33]**Lakota** for 'White man.'

[34]**Placer gold:** Gold, washed into a river from its source, mostly broken small and smoothed by the action of water and silt. Likewise Hard Rock mining produces gold that can be identified as such by opposite characteristics, sharp and jagged pieces broken from the quartz or rock.

[35]**Pokes:** Small, usually leather pouches that can be tied tightly and used for gold dust and nuggets.

[36]**Plews:** Beaver skins.

[38]**Whiteout:** Driven snow, blown by the wind with such ferocity that clear vision, recognised landmarks, or seeing the path ahead becomes impossible.

[39]**Mustang:** Small, wild, hardy ponies that were plentiful on the US Plains, and descended from horses brought by the Spaniards.

[40]**Puncheon:** Split log or post smoothed on one side with an adze. When used for cabin flooring it was strong, stable and long lasting.

[41]**Sutler:** A civilian who was authorised to operate a store on or near an army post or camp. He sold goods and items that were not considered essential for the army to supply to troopers, and fulfilled a very important role in the life of the soldier, more especially in far flung outposts of the frontier.

[42]**Chivington:** John Milton Chivington was a Methodist pastor and a Freemason Grand Master. In November 1864 he led a force of 700 Colorado Territory volunteers in an attack on an Indian camp, Cheyanne and Arapaho, and slaughtered up to 600 souls, two thirds of them women and children and infants. Mutilations then followed, and victim's body parts, including those of women and children, taken as trophies. The Indians were peaceful, and had settled 40 miles north of Fort Lyon to negotiate a surrender, (which was completed successfully). They therefore thought themselves safe. It was a cowardly and wicked slaughter, totally unexpected and merciless.

Although Chivington was found guilty of gross misconduct, he was never punished, and maintained in the rightness of his conduct to his dying day. His later life and subsequent failed marriage to his daughter in law, together with other nefarious dealings, justifies very well the sentiment expressed by the editor of the Omaha Daily Herald, when he tagged Chivington "A rotten clerical hypocrite".

[43]**Spencer Rifle** 1860: The first military metallic cartridge repeating rifle. Lever action, and fed from a magazine tube under the barrel holding 7 rounds, it was capable, in the right hands, of a rate of fire of 14-20 aimed rounds per minute. Compared to the standard muzzle loaders, with a rate of fire of 2-3 rounds per minute, the Spencer represented a very significant tactical advantage. With an effective range of 500 yards, its .52 slug was a force to be reckoned with in battle conditions.

Paradoxically, the Spencer was somewhat before its time. The infrastructure and supply chain of the then military was not effective enough to keep abreast of the needs such a weapon would bring, and forward thinking not advanced enough to utilise it. A common complaint being that the soldiers would be tempted to waste ammunition with such a weapon! The manufacture of more munition supplies, and getting them delivered more quickly, being a major hurdle of the then military command. Consequently, army commanders were slow to capitalise on the tactical value the rifle offered. Like the Gatling machine gun offered to them around the same time by Richard Jordan Gatling, its inventor. They failed to see its advantages also! As so often with military thinking, the passage of time and numerous failures would be needed before they changed the old for the new!

[44]**Jim Bridger:** James Felix Bridger 1804-1881, was a trapper, mountain man, Indian fighter, army scout and guide. Although he is reckoned as one of the foremost frontiersmen of the time, and was conversational in several Indian languages, he was illiterate. Throughout his life he married three Indian wives, two of them Shoshone and one Flathead. Two of them bore him living children, and one died in childbirth. He served as a scout under Colonel B. Carrington, and was at Fort Phil Kearny during the time of Fetterman.

[45]**Puncheon:** Split log or post smoothed on one side with an adze. When used for cabin flooring it was strong, stable and long-lasting.

[47]**Clapboard:** Thin boards overlapping horizontally to close in a barn or outhouse.

[48]**Missouri:** Played a central role in the westward expansion of the US. The Oregon trail, Santa Fe trail and California trail all began in Missouri. It was there also that the unscrupulous fleeced the unwary of their last dollar, pressing upon them goods and 'must have' items for frontier travel. A little further along the trail at Fort Laramie, those same 'must have' items were discarded as the traveller realised his mules or oxen could only pull so much so far, and then lie down! Fort Laramie became known as Fort Sacrifice on account of this offloading and dumping of burdensome and heavy items.

[49]**Soddy:** Small cabin built by cutting large sods of earth and building them like bricks one upon the other. They were warm, snug, and quickly and cheaply raised.

[50]**Chickamauga:** This battle was fought on September 18-20, 1863 between Union and Confederate forces. With Gettysburgh, it was one of two bloodiest battles in the Civil War. Union casualties, killed, wounded and captured, 16,170 men. Confederate casualties, 18,454.

[51]**Hominy grits:** Coarse ground cornmeal boiled in milk or water and served as a stiff porridge. It can be savoury or sweet, depending on the diner's choice, and the availability of the accompaniments!

[52]**Squashes:** Butternut, Pumpkins or such like fruits, usually used and cooked as vegetables.

[53]**Jerky:** Meat, usually buffalo meat, cut into thin strips and dried.

[54]**Hardtack:** A simple mixture of flour and water, sometimes a little salt. It was the cheapest and longest lasting biscuit available, and was for centuries the staple survival food for armies and navies. It was so hard it needed wetted before eating, and was best served in soups or gravies where it absorbed the flavours. Eaten of itself it was extremely bland.

[55]**Sitting Bull:** A highly intelligent and fearless Sioux leader who was to the fore in opposing US government policies toward the Indians.

His defeat of Custer at the Big Horn made him a marked man thereafter. At that time the Ghost Dance, a religious movement, was gaining momentum among the reservation Indians. Although not a War Dance, it nevertheless carried ominous undertones. The Dance was supposed to protect its adherents from bullets, and foretold of the day when all the dead would return to support the remaining Indians in their struggle. The Sioux interpreted this as a means of removing all whites from their lands!

It was inevitable that this movement would prove a catalyst for disaster. Fearful that Sitting Bull would harness the widespread influence of this Ghost Dance to violent ends, the authorities moved to arrest him.

On December 15, 1890, a dawn raid was made on his reservation cabin. A crowd quickly gathered and a young Indian shot a law enforcement officer. In retaliation the Reservation Police opened fire on Sitting Bull, killing him instantly. Many of the reservation Indians fled when this news reached them.

One such group was encountered at Wounded Knee on the Lakota Pine Ridge Indian Reservation. While disarming the group, a deaf mute was reluctant to give up his rifle, and when the weapon discharged it signalled one of the greatest atrocities in US military history up to that time. Around 300 men women and children were massacred.

The snow, stained red with their life's blood, only added to the horror of that day. Four Hotchkiss Mountain guns supplemented the army arsenal. With a 42 mm calibre, and a range far in excess of any small arms or rifles, the poorly clad and hungry band of men women and children, on foot in the snow, would have no hope of escape.

[56]**Old Ned:** A fiction.

[57]**Musselshell:** County in northern Montana.

[58]**Nine Hours:** This actually happened. Even taking into account the possibility of exaggeration, what a sight it must have presented, and what great numbers of buffalo there must have been at that time. Different historians have given the number in many millions.

[59]**Duke:** In January of 1872, the Grand Duke Alexis, third son of the Czar of Russia, was treated to a very expensive hunting trip courtesy of the US Army. Generals Sheridan and Sherman were prominent in their support for the buffalo destruction. The Russians were well provided for. An escort of two companies of infantry, two of cavalry, and a regimental band with teamsters and cooks, boarded a special train of the Union Pacific Railroad for North Platte Nebraska. In five days of wanton waste they killed hundreds of buffalo. Sherman and Sheridan were not alone in this widespread programme of annihilation. It was customary for military commanders to lay on this form of entertainment for distinguished guests.

[60]**Paint ponies:** These can be traced back to the multicoloured horses of early Spanish explorers. They had white spots or splashes on their main colour and were favoured by the Indians.

[62]**Stumping powder:** Explosive mix used for land clearance, tree stumps.

[63]**Sweeper:** Fallen tree overhanging low over a waterway or river, often sweeping canoeists to their deaths, hence the name.

[64]**White water:** A river fast flowing over rocky terrain and causing swift and dangerous passage.

[65]**Pokes:** Small, usually leather pouches that can be tied tightly and used for gold dust and nuggets.

[66]**Wickiups and Wigwams:** They were rounded huts or shelters supported by a frame of saplings or green flexible branches and covered by grass or whatever material was available. They were not carried from place to place like a tepee, but left behind and a new one built in the next location.

[67]**Nu-tsi-pa:** Paiute for 'little bird.'

[68]**Richard Pratt:** In 1879, under government sponsorship, Pratt founded the Carlisle Indian Industrial Boarding school, Pennsylvania. Before he was through many such institutions would be constructed. These were designed to strip away all that the Indian child knew of his or her native upbringing. Language, beliefs, history and heritage.

The institutions were draconian in operation, and physical abuse was rampant. Thousands were to die in these schools and be buried in unmarked graves.

Pratt's philosophy was, 'Kill the Indian, save the man'. This was just one of the many injustices inflicted upon the indigenous people, and the legacy of its abysmal failure is still felt today.

**OTHER TITLES BY THE SAME AUTHOR:**

**From out a Poor Cradle**
A memoir

**Dark Strangers**
Stories from an African Mission

**Fornenst the Glow**
Fireside Tales. Musings from a Parson's Pen

**Fame Mission – The Untold Story**
An Expose

**Changed Times**
Social, Ecclesiastical and Political Corruption in Ulster

**Where Tides Run Deep**
An 1800s Seafaring Adventure

**What a Friend we have in Jesus**
A History of Joseph Scriven

**Are you inspired to write a book?**

Contact

**Maurice Wylie Media**

**Your Inspirational & Christian Book Publisher**

Based in Northern Ireland and distributing around the world.

www.MauriceWylieMedia.com